Bound by Prophecy

The Key Stone Pack Prequel

Aisling Elizabeth

Copyright © 2023 by Aisling Elizabeth

All rights reserved.

No portion of this book may be reproduced in any form without written permission from the publisher or author, except as permitted by U.S. copyright law.

The story, all names, characters, and incidents portrayed in this production are fictitious. No identification with actual persons (living or deceased), places, buildings, and products is intended or should be inferred.

ISBN – 9798858284710

Cover design – Aisling Elizabeth

Dedication

To everyone who isn't expecting a happy ending.

Contents

Acknowledgments	VII
Content Warning	VIII
Chapter 1	1
Chapter 2	7
Chapter 3	16
Chapter 4	25
Chapter 5	34
Chapter 6	43
Chapter 7	49
Chapter 8	57
Chapter 9	64
Chapter 10	72
Chapter 11	82
Chapter 12	89
Chapter 13	99
Chapter 14	107

Chapter 15	117
Chapter 16	123
Bound by Fate	130
About Aisling Elizabeth	132
Also By Aisling Elizabeth	134

Acknowledgments

My first thanks go to my Higher Power Puzzle Pieces, Sydney and Rach. Ladies your support is freaking amazing. And all my other puzzle pieces, I love you all.

My team who have helped to make this book and series (and my life) happen. Kayla, you are so amazing and thanks for getting me drunk food. Ryan, thanks for driving us places, while I probably drive you up the wall. Rach for reminding me that I am brilliant. Britt for giving me the go ahead to do what I want. Amanda and Nicole, you may be new but you are stuck with me now. My British B*tches, Jes and Naomi, who suffer through my constant word count updates, and crazy weird messages and the occasional naughty picture. And to every one of the amazing people who run the book related Facebook groups that have let me post my dribble in, you are giving us authors and readers a chance to connect and it ain't easy to run these groups.

And of course to my wonderful children. Thanks for being you, because no one else could.

CONTENT WARNING

My lovely Puzzle Pieces,

This prequel aims to give a little back story to the series and can be read first, or at any point during the series. I am going to be straight with you from the start. This book will not have a happy ending, not even a happy for now. Sorry. But this book isn't an ending, it is a beginning. I promise you though that, eventually, there will be a happy ending. That being said here are the content warnings for it.

This book contains elements of, or mentions of the following: -
Kidnapping
Manipulation
Coercion
Trauma
Pregnancy (and pregnancy complications)
Violent attacks.
Death

Please make sure that you take care while reading and if you feel I have missed any potential triggers then please reach out to me at aish@aislingelizabeth.com.

A few more things to consider. This prequel is the start of a series that is a re-imagining of a previous series (The Dark Essence World) that I wrote and is no longer available. There will be some common elements but this is most definitely a new story. Also I am English and I write in British English, so if the spelling looks a tad funky it might just be that.

Happy (ish) Reading

Chapter 1

Andriana

The chilly wind bit at my cheeks as I stood before the entrance gates of the Silver Stone pack territory. The massive iron gates loomed above me, adorned with intricate carvings of wolves and vines that twisted around each other like lovers entwined. I hesitated, unsure if I should even be here. I had recently become the priestess of the Lake Key Coven, one of the strongest covens in the UK, after my mother's sudden death. This would be my first act as Priestess, and I couldn't help but feel the weight of responsibility pressing down on my chest.

"Can I really do this?" I murmured to myself, feeling the familiar knot of uncertainty twist in my stomach. "I'm only eighteen."

But I knew I had no choice. The Silver Stone pack was one of the largest known packs, and their alpha, Alpha Declan Anderson, was a decent man who cared for his people. They were counting on me, and I couldn't let them down.

The gates seemed to loom even larger as I hesitated, my doubt threatening to overtake me. Just then, a handsome man appeared from within the territory, striding towards the gates with an air of confidence. His dark hair was tousled, and a mischievous glint sparkled in his eyes. As he approached, he offered me a charming grin that seemed to light up his face.

"Lost, are you?" he asked, his voice warm and friendly. I bristled at the assumption but chose to keep my tone polite.

"No, I've been summoned by Alpha Declan Anderson."

"Ah, so you're the witch," he said, his eyes scanning me up and down. "You look younger than I expected." The comment stung, feeding my insecurities about not being good enough for the role I'd inherited. Annoyance flared within me, and I scowled at him.

"Witches have their powers from a young age. We don't have to wait until our teens to get our gifts like some," I retorted, feeling into his own power and guessing his rank. "I suppose you were sixteen before you got your wolf, like most betas?" Surprise flickered across his face, but he quickly recovered, grinning once more.

"Well, you certainly know your stuff. Yes, I'm Beta Gregg Pierce. It's a pleasure to meet you."

"Likewise," I muttered, my heart still racing from the confrontation. I couldn't afford to let anyone see my vulnerability; I had to project strength and confidence, even if it was just an act.

"Are you coming in or what?" Gregg asked, raising an eyebrow. His mischievous smile still played on his lips, but I could sense a hint of impatience. I nodded with forced confidence, forcing myself to stand tall as the Beta gestured towards a hidden building to the side. As if on cue, the ornate gates before us began to open, creaking softly as they revealed the pathway ahead. I swallowed hard and took my first steps into Silver Stone pack territory, feeling the weight of my new responsibilities bearing down upon me.

Following Gregg, we reached a sleek black car parked a little way down the path. He opened the passenger door for me with a polite nod, and I slid into the leather seat, taking in the scent of the car's interior, it was a mixture of leather and something distinctly wild, like the earth after a rainstorm. Gregg slipped into the driver's seat, starting the engine with a low rumble.

As he drove us through the pack territory, he attempted to make small talk, asking about my journey and if I had any trouble finding the place. But my eyes were drawn to the breathtaking landscape that unfolded around us. Tall trees cast dappled shadows over rolling hills, and in the distance, I could see the shimmering cascade of a waterfall feeding into a river that appeared to wind its way through the territory.

"Beautiful, isn't it?" Gregg remarked, following my gaze.

"Absolutely," I breathed, unable to tear my eyes away from the scene. We continued down the road, which now ran alongside the river, until we reached an old stone bridge. As Gregg expertly guided the car across, I couldn't help but admire the craftsmanship of the structure, it had clearly stood the test of time, much like the pack who called this land home. On the other side of the bridge, we entered a vast park with a large, imposing house at its heart. The building's dark stone facade seemed to hold secrets within its walls, and I felt both curiosity and trepidation stirring within me.

As we got closer, I noticed construction work on either side of the park; the foundations had been laid, but it was still too early in the process to make out what the structures would become. What were they building? And why now?

"Alpha Declan has big plans for the pack," Gregg commented as if reading my thoughts. "He's always looking for ways to improve our home and strengthen our community." His words resonated within me, and I found myself hoping that I could do the same for my own coven. Could I truly be the leader they needed?

Finally, the car came to a stop in front of the grand entrance of the house. Gregg was out of the vehicle in an instant and hurried around to open my door. I stepped out hesitantly, looking around at the people who seemed to be going about their daily lives. They appeared content, and it struck me just how important my role would be in maintaining that happiness.

"Come on," Gregg urged, leading me into the house. We climbed four flights of stairs, each step echoing through the dimly lit hallway. The higher we went, the more oppressive the atmosphere became, and by the time we reached the top floor, I could feel a weight upon my chest.

"Here we are," he said, guiding me down a narrow corridor and into a darkened room. As the door creaked shut behind us, I immediately noticed the smell, a sickening mix of illness and flowers attempting in vain to mask it. My eyes adjusted to the dim light, and I saw a woman lying in a large bed. Her eyes were closed, her pale skin glistening with sweat. Her once lustrous black hair lay tangled and unkempt upon the pillow. Sitting beside her was another woman with dark brown hair and an imposing man, his own dark locks falling over his furrowed brow. He held the hand of the woman in the bed as if it were a lifeline. The atmosphere in the room was heavy with sadness, and I felt a pang of sympathy deep within my heart.

"Is... is she...?" My voice trailed off as my gaze drifted to the woman's swollen belly, realising that she must have been at least six months pregnant.

"Alpha Declan will explain everything," Gregg murmured, his voice barely audible above the soft whispers of sorrow that echoed through the room.

I stood there for a moment, taking in the scene before me, feeling the weight of responsibility settle on my shoulders. Gregg cleared his throat and the man by the bed looked up, his eyes bloodshot and weary. He rose from his seat, his tall frame casting an imposing shadow over the room as he approached us.

"Ah, you must be Andriana," he said, his voice surprisingly gentle despite his tired state. "I am Alpha Declan Anderson, and this is my mate, Luna Fallon." He gestured towards the woman in the bed, his love and concern for her evident in every line of his face.

"Thank you for coming so quickly," he continued, his eyes appraising me with a mixture of hope and desperation. "We've heard great things about your coven's power, and we hope that you can help our Luna."

As he spoke, I couldn't help but notice the strain behind his words, the way his hands clenched and unclenched at his sides. My heart went out to him, it was clear that he was doing everything in his power to save the ones he loved most.

"Since Fallon became pregnant with our firstborn son and heir, she has been... unwell," he explained, his gaze flicking back to the bed. "We have tried every conventional medicine available, but nothing seems to work. At this point, we fear for both her life and that of our child." His words echoed through my mind, and I felt a surge of determination rise within me. This was why I had been called here, and I would do everything in my power to help them. But first, I needed to understand more about what was causing the illness.

"May I?" I asked, gesturing towards the bed. Alpha Declan nodded, stepping aside to allow me access. As I moved closer, I could see the beads of sweat on Luna Fallon's brow and the lines of pain etched into her face. She was fighting a battle within herself, and I knew that it was up to me to provide her with the strength she needed to win.

"Alpha Declan," I said softly, my focus fixed on Luna Fallon, "please tell me more about when her illness began. The more I know, the better equipped I will be to help her." As he relayed the details, I listened intently, filing away each piece of information in my mind. As I did so, I couldn't help but feel the weight of their situation pressing down on me, urging me to find the answers they so desperately needed.

"Your Luna's plight is deeply saddening, Alpha Declan," I said, my voice barely above a whisper. In the dim light of the room, I could see the shadows of exhaustion and grief carving deep into his features, and it stirred something within me. A need to help, to bring some semblance of hope back into this sombre place. "If you don't mind, I'd like to examine her more closely."

"Of course," he replied, his voice strained with worry. "Anything that might help."

Alpha Declan guided me toward the bed where Luna Fallon lay. The woman who had been sitting by her side rose gracefully, casting a worried glance at Luna before joining Beta Gregg. He instinctively wrapped an arm around her as they watched from across the room.

I sat down in the vacant chair next to Luna Fallon, offering her a reassuring smile. Up close, I could see beads of sweat glistening on her pale skin, evidence of the battle she waged within herself. When her eyes fluttered open, they were clouded with pain and fear, making my heart clench with empathy.

"Please," she whispered through cracked lips, her voice barely audible. "Help me."

Taking her cold hand in mine, I closed my eyes and focused on connecting with the essence that flowed within her. The power hidden beneath her fragile exterior pulsed beneath my fingertips, drawing me further into her soul. As I ventured deeper, I found myself nearing the centre of Luna Fallon's being, the sacred space where her unborn child grew. My breath hitched as I sensed the sickness that enveloped them both: dark, sinister chains choking the life force of the child, binding it with an unnatural strength that left me feeling nauseous.

My eyes snapped open, tears blurring my vision as the reality of the situation hit me like a tidal wave. I stared up at Alpha Declan, my chest heaving with the weight of my discovery. His gaze was fixed on me, filled with a desperate hope that I might have the answers he sought.

"Alpha Declan, I am so sorry," I whispered, my voice thick with emotion. "There is a magic curse on your unborn child."

Chapter 2

Andriana

"Charlene, I'll see you soon," I said into the phone, my voice soft yet firm. A flicker of relief coursed through me at the thought of having another witch by my side to help with this dire situation.

"Of course, Andriana. Just be careful, all right?" Charlene's concern was palpable even through the static of our connection.

"Always," I assured her with a tight smile before hanging up. The dim light of Alpha Declan's office seemed to press in around me as I turned to face him. He sat slumped behind his dark oak desk, the weight of his Luna's illness evident in every line of his body. Shadows carved hollows beneath his eyes, and I could feel the strain of his worry like a tangible thing in the air.

"Charlene's on her way," I informed him gently. "She's a seer witch from my coven, she should be able to get a better understanding of the curse than I can."

I watched as something akin to gratitude flickered over his weary features, but it was quickly replaced by exhaustion. It was clear that he needed rest if he was going to be of any use in saving his Luna and their unborn child.

"Alpha Declan, while we wait, why don't you try to get some sleep?" I suggested, trying to infuse my words with both authority and kindness. "You won't be able to help Fallon or the baby if you're running on empty." Beta Gregg, who had been sitting silently on the worn leather sofa, nodded vigorously in agreement.

"Andriana's right, Alpha. You need to take care of yourself, too." Alpha Declan hesitated for a moment, clearly torn between his desire to stay involved and his body's desperate need for rest. But eventually, he nodded and stood, wincing slightly as his muscles protested the movement.

"You'll let me know as soon as Charlene arrives?" he asked, looking from me to Gregg.

"Of course," I promised, and with that, he left the office, his steps heavy with fatigue. I sighed and sank into one of the plush armchairs, feeling the weight of responsibility settle on my shoulders. What if we couldn't break this curse? What if I wasn't strong enough to save the Luna and her child?

Now alone with Beta Gregg, I realised just how truly worried I was for Luna Fallon and her unborn child. The air in the room seemed to thicken, pressing down on me from all sides. Gregg seemed to pick up on my unease, and his expression softened in understanding.

"This has been particularly difficult on Declan," he confessed, his voice weighed down by concern. "He loves Fallon so much, and it kills him to see her suffering like this. It's hard for me too, he's my best friend, and I feel so helpless." I glanced over at him, noting the way his hands clenched into fists as he spoke. The bond between an alpha and his beta was a strong one, forged through years of trust, loyalty, and friendship. It was clear just how much Gregg cared for his pack leader.

"Gregg," I began, my voice laced with determination. "You're not helpless." I reached over and gently placed my hand on his arm, hoping to convey the sincerity in my words. "Your special gift alone is helping Alpha Declan to keep calm through all of this turmoil." His eyes widened, and I could see the shock flickering across his face.

"How did you know about that?" he asked, his voice barely above a whisper. "Nobody knows about my gift. Hell, I don't even know what it is." I smiled softly at him, taking a moment to gather my thoughts before answering.

"I can see faerie in your essence," I finally said, watching as his brow furrowed in confusion. "That's where the gift itself comes from. It's only a small amount, but it's there, and somewhere in your bloodline there was a faerie." He stared at me, his eyes searching mine for any hint of deception. But I held his gaze steadily, wanting him to understand not only the truth of my words but also the depth of my conviction.

"My friend Charlene is the same way," I continued, my voice growing stronger as I spoke. "That's where her seer power comes from, all the way from the three fates themselves."

Gregg's mouth hung open, his shock giving way to awe. He looked at me as if I had just unlocked some secret door within him, revealing a part of his identity that had always remained hidden.

"Wait, so how do you know all of this?" Gregg asked, his curiosity piqued. "I wasn't even sure that faeries and the fates were real." I smiled at him, my eyes twinkling with a hint of mischief.

"Did any of your pack ever attend a magic school?" He shook his head.

"Werewolves tend to keep to themselves. We have our own ways of learning about our powers and abilities."

"Ah," I said, nodding in understanding. "Well, there are magic schools out there, run by the Alchemists. They're the ones who taught me everything I know."

"Alchemists, huh?" Gregg muttered, frowning slightly. "Bunch of elitist pricks." I couldn't help but laugh at his remark.

"They can be," I admitted. "But without them, none of us would exist. They've dedicated their lives to preserving the balance of power among supernatural beings." Also, the little known fact was that the Alchemists were the creators of the supernatural races. It was their essence that ran through our veins and powered our magic. Nobody really knows where the Alchemist came from, apart from the Alchemists themselves obviously, and they were spilling those secrets anytime soon. Gregg looked intrigued, his wolfish eyes absorbing every word I spoke. But before he could ask another question, his expression went blank, and his gaze seemed to lose focus.

"Gregg?" I asked cautiously, concern flooding through me.

"Sorry," he said, blinking rapidly as if coming out of a trance. "I just received a mind link from someone in the pack. Your friend Charlene has arrived."

"Finally," I sighed, relieved. "Let's go meet her."

As we left the office and made our way through the pack house, I couldn't help but feel a mix of excitement and dread. With Charlene's help, we might finally uncover the truth about the curse and find a way to save Luna Fallon and her unborn child. But what if the darkness that surrounded them was too powerful to overcome? What if we were already too late? I pushed those thoughts aside, refusing to let fear take hold. As a priestess of the Lake Key Coven, I had faced countless challenges, and each one had only made me stronger. This time would be no different.

Descending the staircase, my heart raced with anticipation. Gregg and I reached the entrance of the pack house where Charlene stood, her blond hair cascading over her shoulders, a small smile tugging at her lips.

"Char," I breathed, rushing forward to embrace my friend. The familiar scent of lavender and sage enveloped me as we hugged tightly. "I'm so glad you're here."

"Anything for you, Andriana," she replied, her voice warm and reassuring. As we pulled apart, her gaze flickered to Gregg, offering him a polite nod. "You must be Beta Gregg. It's nice to finally meet you."

"Likewise," Gregg replied, his tone guarded but respectful.

"Let's head up to Luna Fallon's room. Alpha Declan is waiting for us there," I said, guiding them towards the stairs. With each step, I could feel the weight of the situation pressing down on me, clouding the air with tension and unease.

Reaching the fourth floor, we found Alpha Declan standing in front of the bedroom door, his expression weary but determined. His eyes met mine briefly before shifting to Charlene.

"Thank you for coming," he said, his voice low and strained.

"Of course, Alpha. I'll do everything I can to help," Charlene assured him, her serenity a stark contrast to the turmoil that roiled within the rest of us. We stepped into the dimly lit bedroom where Luna Fallon slept, her chest rising and falling in shallow breaths. The sight of her fragile form was like a punch to the gut, reminding me of the urgency of our task.

"Charlene," I began, my voice barely above a whisper, "I've seen energetic chains wrapped around the life force of the unborn baby. They're draining energy from both mother and child." My hands trembled as I recounted the horrifying details, my heart aching for the life that was slipping through our fingers. Charlene's eyes widened in shock, her lips pressed into a thin line.

"I've never encountered something like this before," she admitted, her voice heavy with concern. "This curse is incredibly powerful, Andriana," she said, her voice hushed and urgent. "I saw it casting its darkness over the whole pack as I arrived." She moved to sit at a table near the edge of the room, far from the slumbering Luna. I noticed the Beta give her a strange look, and she smiled.

"The stronger the power, the more confusing things get for me," she explained, her fingers idly tracing the wooden surface.

"Oh," he replied. "I would think that the more power means better." Charlene rolled her eyes.

"Not when there is so much that it's like trying to have six different conversations in my head at once," she scoffed. I knew that she was tense with what she was going to have to do, so she was more snappy than usual. Gregg raised an eyebrow at her reaction and then looked at me.

"Sounds like you witches are a feisty bunch."

"Only when we need to be," I said with a wink.

Charlene pulled a black crystal scrying ball from her bag. She set it carefully on the table, the orb shimmering with untold possibilities.

"Take my hand," I instructed Charlene, reaching out to her. When Gregg looked at us quizzically, I explained, "I'm acting as her anchor so she doesn't get lost in the visions." Charlene took a deep breath, muttering incantations under her breath. As she spoke, I could see the invisible walls she had erected around herself crumbling away. It was a necessary step, but it left her vulnerable, a fact that sent a shiver down my spine.

"Are you ready?" I asked softly, my heart pounding in my chest.

"Always," she replied, her eyes meeting mine with steely determination. As she peered into the depths of the scrying ball her eyes turned black, her gaze locked onto the scrying ball as if she were staring into the abyss. I felt our connection strengthen, anchoring her to this plane of existence. The world around us receded, leaving only the swirling vortex of magic and the weight of our shared responsibility. Time seemed to lose all meaning as Charlene explored the shadowy recesses of the curse, her eyes glazed over with the intensity of her vision. But through the anchor, I could feel her strength and resolve as she navigated the tangled web of darkness. I held my breath, feeling a mix of anxiety and awe at the sight before me. The room fell silent, the air heavy with anticipation.

"Wait," I whispered, more to myself than anyone else, as I tightened my grip on Charlene's hand. I could feel the power coursing through her veins, and I knew that our connection was the only thing keeping her tethered to reality. Every so often, her body would twitch involuntarily, and I couldn't help but wonder what horrors she was witnessing within the depths of the curse. Time seemed to stretch on forever, each second ticked by like an eternity. I focused on maintaining our link, offering silent support to my friend as she plunged deeper into the darkness. And then, suddenly, I felt a sharp tug on my hand – the signal to pull her back from the brink.

"Charlene!" I called out, reaching into her mind and pulling on her essence with all my might. She gasped, her body slumping in the chair as she struggled to catch her breath. Tears streamed down her face as she turned to me, her expression a mix of fear and sorrow.

"Adriana," she choked out, her voice barely a whisper. "It's... really bad."

Charlene took a breath and wiped her eyes with a hand. Gregg handed her a glass of water and she drank from it quickly, draining the whole glass. After taking a few moments to regain her composure, she pulled a worn leather-bound book from her bag and began feverishly scribbling down words and images. My curiosity piqued, I leaned in closer, catching glimpses of chains, a dagger, and the words 'night', 'death', and 'wolf'.

"Charlene, what does this mean?" I asked, my voice laced with concern. The gravity of the situation was beginning to weigh heavily on me, and I needed answers.

"Give me a moment," she replied, her eyes never leaving the pages of her book. "I need to make sense of it all."

As she continued her frantic writing, I sat quietly, watching the rise and fall of the Luna's chest as she slept. Charlene suddenly looked up at me with more tears shining in her eyes. She looked up at the Alpha, who was waiting expectantly.

"Can we go somewhere else?" Charlene asked. "I need to clear my head." The Alpha nodded, and he led us out of the room and down the hall.

"Charlene, can you tell us more now?" The Alpha's voice was soft but urgent as he led us into the living space on the same floor. The room was warm and inviting with plush sofas and a crackling fire in an ornate hearth. It seemed so at odds with the heavy darkness that clung to our hearts.

"Alright," Charlene sighed, sitting down on one of the sofas, her eyes still slightly glazed from the vision. I sat beside her, ready to offer support, while the Alpha and his Beta perched on the edge of their seats across from us.

"I haven't seen work like this before. It's extremely potent. Whoever the witch is... they're powerful beyond measure."

"Who would do such a thing?" The Alpha's voice trembled with barely restrained emotion. "Why?" Charlene hesitated, looking at me for reassurance. I nodded, and she took a steadying breath.

"It's a blood curse. Someone lost their life for this to happen. Any magic where a life is taken... it's seriously dark." She paused, swallowing hard. "They placed the curse in the name of betrayal, and it reeks of jealousy. The cursed blood is connected to the night and even more darkness. You must know who the person responsible is." As the full implication of Charlene's words sunk in, I could feel the tension in the room thicken. The Alpha clenched his fists, his jaw tightening as his wolf fought to break through.

"Betrayal," the Alpha whispered, his voice strained. The Alpha's rage flared, as destructive and uncontrollable as a storm. With a guttural growl, he seized the nearest cup, hurling it against the wall with a force that sent shards of porcelain flying like shrapnel. Charlene and I instinctively recoiled, our hearts pounding in sync with the frenetic rhythm of the Alpha's fury.

"Damn Felix! That bloody bastard just can't let go, can he?" The words poured out in a torrent, raw and unfiltered. Charlene eyed me nervously, her lips pressed into a tight line, while I tried to summon my courage to face the tempest before us.

But it was Gregg who stepped forward, his movements fluid and graceful even in the midst of chaos. In seconds, he was by the Alpha's side, his hand firm on the man's shoulder. As if drawn by an invisible force, my eyes locked onto the point of contact, where the Beta's gift manifested in a shimmer of ethereal light. It was as though the very air around them rippled with unseen currents, and I watched, awestruck, as the rage drained from the Alpha like water through a sieve.

"Declan," Gregg murmured, his voice soft yet strong, "I know you're furious, but we need to think this through." The Alpha sank onto the sofa, the fire in his eyes now replaced by a dull, smouldering ember. He looked up at Gregg, his voice hoarse but resolute.

"This... This is an act of war." Gregg nodded solemnly, his brow furrowed in thought.

"I agree, but we don't stand a chance against them. Going after Felix head-on would be playing right into his hands." As they spoke, my mind whirled with the implications of what Charlene had revealed. A blood curse, fuelled by jealousy and darkness, threatened to rip the Silver Stone pack apart from within. The enemy was cunning and powerful, with a mind twisted by bitter resentment. And it fell upon me to stand against that darkness, to protect the innocent lives at stake.

"Sorry for my outburst," Alpha Declan murmured, his previous anger replaced by a quiet exhaustion. He turned to me and Charlene, his gaze apologetic. "There is another alpha, Felix Blackwood, the Alpha of the Shadow Night pack, who is likely behind this. He... had a thing for Fallon, but she refused to join his pack." I had heard of the Shadow Night pack, along with the Silver Stone pack and the Half Moon pack, it was one of the biggest in the country. I only knew so much about the local packs because a former coven witch and friend Becca had met her fated mate at the Half

Moon pack. He was a Gamma werewolf, and she had chosen to move to the pack to be with him, much to the dislike of the general witch community.

"Things got worse when Fallon and I met and discovered we were fated mates," Alpha Declan continued, his voice growing heavy with sorrow. "Felix has been jealous ever since, despite having found his own fated mate and fathering a child." Gregg, who had remained quietly supportive, spoke up.

"The mysterious death of Felix's mate and the news of Fallon's pregnancy could have pushed him over the edge." I watched as Charlene sank into a nearby chair, her eyes fixed on the floor. Her expression was clouded with concern, and I couldn't help but worry about the implications of her visions.

"Charlene?" I asked gently, placing a hand on her shoulder. "What's wrong?" She looked up at me, her eyes filled with sadness.

"The magic is potent, Andriana. It's very likely that Felix had his own mate sacrificed as part of the curse." My heart clenched at the thought of such a vile act, one that went against everything I believed in as a witch. The air in the room seemed to grow heavier, tainted by the darkness of Felix's intentions.

But I knew that there was more to this, and from the look on my friends face, it wasn't good.

"Charlene," I said, my voice trembling as the reality of the situation sank in. "What else did you see?" She hesitated for a moment, her eyes clouded with pain and fear before she spoke up.

"The curse is designed to balance life, Andriana... The other alpha, Felix, will be able to bring life back to his mate by taking the life force from Fallon and Declan's child." Gasps filled the room as we all tried to process the horrifying revelation. The atmosphere grew dense with an ominous energy, threatening to suffocate us.

"He purposely killed his own mate so he could bring her back to life and take the life of Fallon and Declan's son," Charlene added, her voice barely above a whisper. "The curse will kill Luna Fallon and her unborn baby when he is born."

Chapter 3

Andriana

The air in the room was thick with tension, as if it were a tangible force trying to choke us. The revelation hung over our heads like an ominous cloud, threatening to unleash a storm of fury and despair. Charlene's words echoed in my mind, "Luna Fallon and her unborn child will die when he is born." A curse so cruel, I could hardly comprehend it. Alpha Declan paced the length of the room, his hands clenched into fists, veins bulging from his neck and arms as he tried to control the rage inside him. His eyes, filled with a fire that could rival the sun, locked onto mine for a moment before looking away.

"Felix Blackwood," he growled, the name tasting bitter on his tongue. "I should've known that bastard would stoop this low. I want to declare war on the Shadow Night pack."

"Alpha Declan," I said softly, placing a hand on his arm to calm him. "We need to focus on finding a way to break the curse first. We can't risk Luna Fallon and the baby." My heart ached at the thought of their impending fate. Beta Gregg stood near the window, his gaze distant and troubled. He nodded solemnly in agreement.

"Andriana is right. We must put our energy into saving them first." Charlene, her expression grave and pained, stepped closer.

"We will do everything we can to help, Alpha. You have my word."

My thoughts raced as I considered the implications of such a vicious curse. It would take a witch of immense power to weave such dark magic, and that knowledge sent shivers down my spine. As powerful as I was, the idea of facing a witch capable of cursing an entire family to their deaths both intrigued and terrified me.

"Alpha Declan," I began, my voice firm and resolute. "Every witch has their own unique signature hidden within their spells or curses, like a secret code or key. If we can work out the witch's signature, then we should be able to unlock the curse." The room seemed to hold its breath as I spoke, the air thick with anticipation. I could see the glimmer of hope in Alpha Declan's eyes, mixed with the ever-present smouldering fury.

"Then let's find this witch," he growled, his hands gripping the edge of the table so tightly that his knuckles turned white.

"Give me a moment," I said, stepping away from the group and pulling out my phone. My fingers trembled slightly as I dialled the number for the High Priestess of the UK witches, Mirriam Willowvane.

"Hello?" a familiar voice answered, causing my heart to leap into my throat.

"Gayle?" I stuttered, momentarily thrown off by hearing my old friend instead of the High Priestess. "I was trying to reach your mother."

"Mother is at the Alchemist Conclave on official business at the moment," Gayle explained, her tone bright and eager. "But I can help you in her place, Andriana. What do you need?"

"Gayle, we're facing a serious situation here. There's a dark curse that threatens the life of Luna Fallon, of the Silver Stone pack, and her unborn child. We need to find the witch responsible for it. Your mother would have a list of any witches capable of such a curse, right?" My voice trembled with urgency as I spoke, the gravity of our predicament weighing heavily on my mind. Gayle's usually bubbly demeanour seemed to dampen as she realised the seriousness of my request.

"Ew, werewolves," she said, her voice not hiding her disgust. "Is it not enough that one of your coven has already defected because of one of those mutts, now you want to help them." I sighed at her bias. I knew that the majority of the supernatural community had a bias against one or more of other species. Most of the community tried to work together, which was why we had the magic schools in the first place, but the isolation of the shifters caused a lot of the other supernaturals to be cautious of them. Or in some cases, downright rude.

"Gayle," I scolded, "A life is a life, regardless of your personal feelings, now are you going to help or not." I didn't really have time for her bullshit today.

"Of course, Andriana," she replied. I could practically hear the sulking in her voice. "I'll do everything in my power to help you. Just give me a moment to look through our records."

As Gayle rifled through the coven's records, I could hear the rustling of papers and the distant sound of her breathing. My own breaths came shallow and quick, my heart thundering in my chest as I waited for any scrap of information that could lead us to the witch responsible for the curse. Although my concerns of involving the High Priestess's daughter weighed on my mind.

"Gayle, I appreciate your help, but are you sure you're up for this?" I asked hesitantly. The memory of Gayle's wild days at the magic school still lingered in my mind, and I couldn't shake the concern that she might be too eager to prove herself. She also was bitter about me getting the Priestess title of my own coven when my mother died. Like me being the youngest priestess meant that she failed at being the best or something.

"Of course, Andriana!" Gayle exclaimed with a laugh. "Honestly, there aren't many witches on the list who could even come close to casting a curse like this. In fact," she paused for dramatic effect, "the closest one would probably be you!"

"Gayle," I warned, my voice low and stern. "This is not the time for jokes."

"Sorry, sorry," she replied, all traces of amusement gone from her voice. "I know this is serious. But trust me, none of the names here are powerful enough, and cruel enough, to create such a vicious curse."

"Then we'll just have to keep looking," I said, determination settling within me once more. "We'll find the witch responsible and break this curse."

"Actually, why don't I come up and help?" Gayle suggested suddenly. "Three witches are better than two, right?"

"Gayle, you don't have to—" I began, but she cut me off.

"I'm bored anyway, and you know how much I love a good challenge," she insisted, her voice filled with excitement. She didn't give me any time to argue before hanging up the phone.

"Gayle is coming up to help," I told Charlene, whose face immediately fell. It was clear that she wasn't thrilled about the idea, but she held her tongue, knowing that we needed all the help we could get.

The pack house loomed before us as Gayle arrived, her blond hair glowing like sunlight in the fading light. Charlene and I exchanged wary glances, silently acknowledging our shared apprehension.

"Let's get started," Gayle declared, striding into the house with purpose. As we gathered around a worn wooden table, laden with ancient tomes and sacred artefacts, the weight of the task at hand settled heavily upon us. Charlene's gift had revealed that the curse was rooted in energy transference, feeding on the very life force of Luna Fallon and her child. Yet something about it felt amiss, even two lives shouldn't have been enough to power such a potent spell.

"I think we'll need to perform a ritual," I said, determination burning within me. "We must see the strings of the curse, find the witch's signature, and dismantle this dark magic."

"Be cautious," Charlene warned. "Luna is already weak from the curse's effect. We can't go too deep without causing her pain."

"Understood," I replied, nodding solemnly. The Alpha looked at us, his eyes full of worry and barely contained rage, but he trusted us enough to give his permission.

"Please, be careful," he implored.

As we surrounded the weakened Luna, her shallow breaths filled the dimly lit room. The flickering candlelight cast a warm glow on her pale face, the shadows concealing the pain in her eyes. I glanced at Gayle and Charlene, their expressions resolute.

"Let's begin," I whispered, my voice wavering slightly. Together, we closed our eyes and began to sink into our ritual state. Our minds reached out towards the curse, feeling for its dark tendrils coiled around Luna's life force. As we delved deeper, the curse unfurled before us like an intricate tapestry of complex strings, each vibrating with their own sinister energy.

"Be careful," I reminded myself, as well as Gayle and Charlene. "We can't push her too far." Despite the caution, I couldn't help but marvel at the complexity of the curse woven around Luna. It was a malicious masterpiece, designed to not only take lives but also cause immense suffering. As we continued to explore the threads of dark magic, I noticed something peculiar, the strings seemed to travel outwards, away from Luna's body, branching off in many directions.

"Gayle, Charlene," I called out mentally, "do you see this? The curse is drawing energy from multiple sources."

"By the Goddess," Charlene whispered in our shared mental space, her tone awed and fearful. "It's feeding on the whole pack."

"Let's pull back," I suggested, concern mounting for Luna's fragile state. "We've seen enough."

With great effort, we withdrew from the curse, our minds untangling from its dark embrace. As we returned to the physical world, I gasped for air, sweat dripping down my forehead. We were all exhausted, but there was no time for rest. The Luna, too, looked drained, beads of sweat glistening on her skin as she panted in pain. Charlene and Gayle immediately set to work, mixing a potion of herbs designed to alleviate her suffering and bolster her strength.

"Alpha," I said, my voice heavy with the weight of our discoveries. "The curse isn't just on Luna and the child. It's feeding on the entire pack." His eyes widened, his hands clenched into fists at his sides.

"What do you mean?"

"Whenever the baby is born," I continued, struggling to maintain eye contact. "The whole pack will lose something vital, their essence." From across the room, Charlene called out, her voice strained from her efforts.

"Their wolves," she clarified, stirring the potion with a steady hand. "They'll lose their wolves." The Alpha stared at us, his face a mask of disbelief and suppressed rage. "We must find a way to break this curse, no matter what it takes."

I could see the fear and uncertainty in Alpha Declan's eyes as he absorbed what I had told him about the curse. The weight of responsibility for his pack bore down on him, and that they would all suffer because of this malevolent magic was almost too much to bear.

"Tell me, Andriana," he said, his voice heavy with emotion. "Do you know what happens to a werewolf when they lose their wolf essence?"

"Unfortunately, I do," I replied sombrely. When a werewolf loses its wolf essence, it will either kill the vessel, meaning the human side, or send it insane. The Alpha's face contorted with anguish.

"These are my people... My family..."

"Alpha, I'm afraid it gets worse," I continued gently, hating to be the bearer of such terrible news. "From what we found during the ritual, the curse is using the werewolf bond as well as the blood bond. This means that anyone related to the child by blood, pack, or bond will suffer." The Alpha's fists clenched at his sides, his body trembling with barely contained rage.

"My brother, who is the Alpha of the Rose Moon pack, has a son..." His voice cracked, and he swallowed hard before continuing. "Will they also be affected by the curse?"

"Given the nature of the curse, it is highly likely that they will be," I confirmed, my heart aching for him.

"Damn Felix Blackwood and his jealousy!" he snarled. "If only we could break this curse!"

"Alpha, while we were unable to find the witch's signature, we did manage to understand parts of the curse," I offered hesitantly, trying to provide some hope amidst the despair. "We might not be able to break it completely, but we can alter it."

"Alter it?" He looked at me, his eyes searching for any glimmer of hope. "How?"

"By delaying the effects of the curse," I explained. "We could give it a new deadline, say, thirty years from now. That would give us more time to find a way to break it completely."

"Thirty years..." he murmured, contemplating the possibility. "It's not ideal, but it's better than what we're facing now."

"Exactly," I agreed. "It's not a permanent solution, but it will buy us time to find one."

"Then let's do it," he said with determination, his jaw set in resolve. "We'll save my family and my pack, no matter what it takes."

"Very well, Alpha," I nodded, gathering Charlene and Gayle to begin the process of altering the curse. As we worked together, our combined power weaving through the strands of dark magic, I couldn't help but feel a renewed sense of purpose. We might not be able to break the curse yet, but in giving it a new deadline, we had bought ourselves a fighting chance.

We went back into a combined vision to replay the information that we had gathered. Charlene studied the intricate web of the curse with furrowed brows, her eyes following the shimmering threads as they twisted and turned.

"There are many complexities to this curse," she said, her voice soft yet firm. "It seems to disappear entirely in some places before reappearing elsewhere. But the basis is always the bond." I looked at the pulsating strands, each one carrying a weight that pressed against my heart. The bond, that was the key. If we could somehow trigger the release through it, perhaps there was still hope for Luna Fallon and her child. I shared my thoughts with Charlene and Gayle, who nodded in agreement. We dropped back into reality, the grave situation pressing heavily on our minds.

"Let's do some more research," I suggested. "If we can find a way to add a trigger event, we might be able to break the curse."

We spent hours poring over ancient texts and scrolls, exchanging theories and ideas, our fingers stained with ink and dust. The room filled with the scent of burning candles mixed with the musty aroma of old parchment. Finally, we discovered an incantation that seemed promising.

"Listen to this," I said, reading aloud the words written in an elegant, flowing script. "It speaks of a powerful force capable of counteracting dark magic, love."

"Love?" Alpha Declan raised an eyebrow, his anger momentarily forgotten. "How can love break such a vicious curse?"

"True love, specifically," I clarified. "If the child finds their mate, someone they share a deep, genuine bond with, the curse will be broken. But it must be real, not something arranged or forced. It is the act of newly bonded love that can counteract the negativity of the curse." Determination flared in Alpha Declan's eyes. "Like the fated mate bond?" he asked. "There is no bond stronger than that." I smiled and nodded.

"Yes, the fated mate bond would be your best bet, but as long as the love is true it could also be a chosen mate."

"Well, let's do it then," The Alpha said, a new determined glimmer of hope in his eyes.

And so, Charlene, Gayle, and I set to work on altering the curse. Sweat beaded on our foreheads as we chanted and gestured, weaving our magic together to create a new pattern within the dark tapestry. It was painstaking work, but with each passing hour, we could sense the subtle shifts in the curse's structure. Finally, after what felt like an eternity, we completed the ritual. I turned to Alpha Declan, my voice shaky but triumphant.

"We've done it. The curse is now delayed until the child's thirtieth birthday."

"Thank you," he breathed, relief washing over his face. "And if the child finds their true mate before then?"

"Then the curse will be broken for good," I confirmed, praying that this small glimmer of hope would be enough to save them all. "But remember, the bond must be genuine. Cheating or manipulation will only strengthen the curse."

"Understood," he nodded gravely. "You have my eternal gratitude, Andriana."

Chapter 4

Andriana

The sun was just beginning to show at the edge of the horizon, casting an eerie glow over Lake Key Coven as we returned. Charlene, Gayle, and I made our way along the winding path, the gratitude of Alpha Declan still lingering in the air. Luna Fallon's face had already begun to regain its colour, a testament to our success in working on the curse.

"Gayle," I said, my voice softening with concern, "you should stay with me for the next day or so. You need time to recover from all the energy you expended tonight."

"Are you sure?" Gayle asked, her blue eyes searching mine for any sign of hesitation. "I don't want to impose."

"Of course, I'm sure," I insisted, giving her a reassuring smile. "My home is your home."

We reached my house, a small detached Victorian manor that once belonged to my mother. The scent of ivy and roses enveloped us as we approached the front door. With a flick of my wrist, the lock clicked open, and we stepped inside.

"Let me show you to the guest room," I said, leading her up the grand staircase, the wooden steps creaking beneath our feet. I opened the door to a cosy room adorned with vintage wallpaper and plush furnishings. "I hope this will be comfortable for you."

"Thank you, Andriana," Gayle said warmly, her gaze sweeping over the room. "This is more than enough." As I turned to leave, Gayle's voice stopped me.

"Andriana... I don't think the issue is resolved. I have a bad feeling about all of this." I sighed, resting my hand on the doorframe.

"I know what you mean. But let's hope it's just the negative energy lingering around from the curse. We can look into it tomorrow after we've rested."

"Alright," she agreed hesitantly. "Goodnight, Andriana."

"Goodnight, Gayle." I retreated to my own room, the unease settling in the pit of my stomach like a heavy stone. As I changed into my nightclothes and climbed into bed, I couldn't shake the feeling that things were far from being completely resolved. Yet, the exhaustion from the night's events soon overtook me, pulling me into a restless slumber.

The sound of insistent knocking jolted me from my troubled sleep, immediately setting my nerves on edge. I blinked my eyes open, disoriented by the abrupt awakening. The sun was now high in the sky, casting a golden glow through the sheer curtains that billowed softly in the breeze.

"Damn it," I muttered, tossing my blankets aside as I swung my legs over the side of the bed. My heart raced with anxiety, my instincts telling me something wasn't right. As I hurried down the stairs, I tried to shake off the lingering tendrils of unease that clung to me like cobwebs.

"Coming!" I called out, trying to sound composed even as my pulse pounded in my ears. I pulled the front door open and found Stephen, one of the coven members, standing there, his brow furrowed with concern.

"Stephen, what's going on?"

"Good afternoon, Andriana," he said, shifting nervously on his feet. "I'm sorry to disturb you, but there's a man at the Moot Hall looking for you."

"Who is he?" I asked cautiously, my worry mounting.

"I don't know," Stephen admitted. "But he's very persistent, and I have a bad feeling about him."

"Alright, give me a moment to get dressed and we'll go together," I told him, my mind already racing with possibilities. Who could this stranger be, and what could he want with me?

As I turned to head back upstairs, Gayle emerged from the guest room, her blue eyes wide with alarm.

"Andriana, what's happening?"

"Someone's looking for me at the Moot Hall," I explained quickly. "We're going to see who it is."

"Count me in," she declared, her jaw set with determination. We both retreated to our respective rooms, hastily changing into more presentable attire. As I dressed, my thoughts spiralled with worry and curiosity. This visitor had arrived too soon on the heels of our recent ordeal – it couldn't be a coincidence.

"Ready?" I called out to Gayle as I emerged from my room, smoothing down my light red hair.

"Let's do this," she replied, her expression fierce. Together, we strode down the stairs and joined Stephen at the door, prepared to face whatever lay in store for us at the Moot Hall. Ten minutes later, the three of us made our way down the short path to the Moot Hall. The sun had risen high in the sky, casting a warm glow on the cobbled pathway. I greeted passing witches with a friendly smile, receiving waves and nods in return. It warmed my heart to know that I was well-liked within my community.

"Any idea who this man might be?" Gayle asked, her eyes scanning our surroundings as if expecting an ambush.

"None," I replied, my stomach knotting with unease. "But we'll find out soon enough."

As we entered the Moot Hall, the musty smell of old books and potion ingredients filled my nostrils. Standing in the entrance hallway was the man in question. At first glance, he looked slightly intimidating with sharp but handsome features. His black hair was cut short, and his vivid blue eyes seemed to pierce through me. I instantly felt a significant amount of power radiating from him, and I knew without a doubt that he was a sorcerer.

"Good afternoon," he said, his gaze locked onto mine as he extended a hand. "My name is Myron Tressier." I shook his hand cautiously, feeling the energy crackling between us like electricity.

"Andriana Moorland," I replied, trying to maintain a polite and friendly demeanour despite my growing apprehension. "What brings you here?"

"Ah, straight to the point," Myron noted with a faint smirk. "I have been travelling around the country, and I've heard whispers of your talents, Andriana. I couldn't resist coming to see for myself."

"Whispers?" I asked, raising an eyebrow. "From whom?"

"Let's just say there are many who speak highly of you," he replied enigmatically, his eyes flickering briefly to Gayle and Stephen before returning to me. Gayle shifted uncomfortably beside me, obviously feeling the weight of his gaze.

"What exactly do you want, Mr Tressier?" she asked, her voice strained.

"Perhaps we could discuss this somewhere more private," Myron suggested, his eyes never leaving mine. I hesitated for a moment, weighing my options. I didn't trust him, but I couldn't afford to turn away any potential allies, or enemies, without first understanding their intentions. With a nod, I agreed, leading him deeper into the Moot Hall with Gayle and Stephen flanking me on either side.

"I've heard so much about you and your coven, Andriana," Myron Tressier said, his voice smooth like honey. His smile was disarming, but I knew better than to drop my guard.

"Thank you, Mr Tressier," I replied cautiously, trying to mask my unease. "Would you care to join us for some tea in the sunroom?"

"Tea sounds delightful, thank you," he agreed, falling into step beside me as Gayle and Stephen trailed behind.

The sunroom was a sanctuary within the Moot Hall, its walls of glass allowing sunlight to pour in and warm the room. We settled into one of the window booths, where we could watch the other witches bustling about in the garden outside.

"Your coven has quite a lovely home here," Myron commented, casting an appreciative eye over the lush greenery surrounding us.

"Thank you," I said, pouring tea for each of us. The fragrant steam curled through the air as I handed him his cup. "We take great pride in our little corner of the world."

"Speaking of which," I continued, taking a sip of my tea and watching him closely. "What brings you to Lake Key? You mentioned travelling around the country?"

"Indeed," Myron smiled, cradling his teacup between his long, elegant fingers. "I'm exploring the magical communities before starting my postgraduate studies. It's been an enlightening journey so far."

"Ah, I see," I said, interested despite my reservations. "And what drew you to our coven specifically?"

"Last night, I felt an incredible surge of energy," Myron explained, fixing his piercing blue eyes on me. "It was unlike anything I've ever experienced. I couldn't resist meeting the witch capable of such power." A shiver ran down my spine at his words, but I tried to remain composed. "I'm honoured that our work caught your attention," I said, feeling the weight of Gayle's and Stephen's gazes on me.

"Your abilities are truly extraordinary, Andriana" Myron said, his eyes never wavering from mine. "I believe there is much we could learn from one another." As he spoke, a thousand questions raced through my mind. What did he truly want? Could I trust him? And what would happen if I allowed this enigmatic sorcerer into my life?

I glanced at Gayle, noting her wide-eyed fascination with Myron. She seemed completely enamoured by him, hanging on his every word. Rolling my eyes, I gestured to Stephen, who had been hovering nearby, to fetch Charlene.

"Tell me, Myron," I said, trying to regain control of the conversation. "How did you know it was someone from our coven?" Myron's lips curled into an amused smile as he regarded me.

"Oh, I don't just know it was someone from your coven. I know it was you, Andriana Moorland." Gayle bristled beside me, her cheeks flushing a deep red.

"It wasn't just Andriana! I was there too!" she blurted out, clearly seeking recognition for her part in our powerful spell. I shot her a subtle look, willing her to be quiet, but she seemed oblivious to my silent plea. We didn't need Myron knowing any more about us than he already did.

As if on cue, Charlene entered the sunroom, her gaze narrowing suspiciously upon Myron. He clapped his hands together and flashed her a charming grin.

"Ah, this must be the seer I've heard so much about," he mused. "I could feel your power as well." While I appreciated his attempt at flattery, I couldn't shake the unsettling feeling that Myron had ulterior motives. My suspicions only grew as Gayle became increasingly flustered by his apparent disinterest in her magical abilities.

"My mother is the High Priestess, you know," she huffed, crossing her arms defensively over her chest.

"Is that so?" Myron replied, nodding politely but seemingly unimpressed by her declaration. His gaze remained fixed on me, making it abundantly clear where his true interest lay.

"Alright," I said, trying to maintain a sense of control over the conversation. "Enough about our powers; why are you really here, Myron?" He leaned back in his chair, a glint of mischief in his vivid blue eyes.

"I'm glad you asked, Andriana," he replied, taking a sip of his tea. "You see, I am aware of a prophecy, a very powerful one. As soon as I felt your power last night, I knew that you were a part of it."

A shiver ran down my spine. Prophecies weren't something to be taken lightly in our world, and the thought of being connected to one made me uneasy.

"Go on," I prompted cautiously. Myron set down his cup and leaned forward, his gaze locked on mine.

"Together, we could work on this prophecy and change the world, Andriana," he said earnestly.

"Change the world?" I scoffed, unable to keep a note of disbelief from my voice. "That's a bold claim to make, especially coming from a stranger."

"Yet, it's true," he insisted, a confident smile playing on his lips. "With your abilities and mine combined, we would be unstoppable." I shook my head firmly, my red hair swaying around my face.

"Thank you for the offer, but I must decline," I told him, struggling to keep my voice steady. "I'm working on building my position as Priestess for now." Myron didn't seem fazed by my rejection. He merely shrugged and finished his drink, his eyes never leaving mine.

"I understand, Andriana," he said softly. "But know that I hope to find a way to convince you to reconsider working with me. We could truly be quite the powerhouse together."

"Thanks, but no thanks," I repeated, trying my best to sound polite yet firm.

With a cheesy, sweeping bow, Myron excused himself from the sunroom. Stephen, who had been hovering near the door, stepped forward and offered to escort him from the coven territory. As they left, I couldn't help but feel a mixture of relief and unease wash over me. What did Myron's arrival mean for me and my coven? And what was this prophecy he spoke of?

Gayle's blonde hair swayed gently as she stood up, her blue eyes darting nervously towards the door.

"I need to use the bathroom," she muttered before slipping out of the sunroom. Charlene immediately took the vacant seat beside me, concern etched across her delicate features. Her usually serene demeanour seemed agitated.

"Andriana," she whispered, leaning in close. "There's something off about Myron. I have a very bad feeling about him." Her intuition had never been wrong before, and my own unease gnawed at the pit of my stomach.

"I feel it too," I admitted, my voice barely audible. "I'll put out some inquiries about him, see what we can find."

"Good idea," Charlene nodded, relief flickering in her eyes for a moment. The sound of the sunroom door creaking open caught our attention, and Stephen walked back in, looking puzzled. His confusion only heightened my suspicions.

"Stephen," I questioned, raising an eyebrow. "Why are you here? Weren't you supposed to be escorting Myron from the coven?" He frowned, rubbing his forehead as if trying to clear his thoughts.

"I thought I was, but then Gayle came over and said she'd do it instead."

"Gayle?" I echoed, incredulous. There was no way she would willingly offer to escort someone like Myron. Glancing at Charlene, I could tell she shared my disbelief.

"Did you actually allow that?" I pressed, searching Stephen's face for any clues.

"Of course not," he protested, his voice rising slightly. "I mean, I can't imagine why I would... But I did." He looked genuinely baffled. My heart raced as I focused my energy on Stephen, seeking answers. A faint residue of foreign magic clung to his aura; someone else's signature mixed with his own. My blood ran cold.

"Stephen, you've been spelled."

"By Myron..." Charlene breathed, understanding dawning in her eyes.

"Exactly," I murmured, my hands clenched into fists. I stood up and quickly made my way through the Moot Hall to the front entrance. Myron and Gayle were standing there talking. I could tell that Gayle was attempting to flirt with Myron. He looked up at me and smiled.

"Changed your mind already?" he asked, a hopeful look in his eye. I narrowed my eyes and walked towards the two of them.

"Excuse me Myron," I said with forced politeness, "But I believe Stephen was showing you out." Myron glanced behind me at a still confused Stephen and then waved his hand towards Gayle.

"Ah yes, but the young Miss Willowvane here wanted a word in my ear," he said. I eyed him suspiciously and then looked over at Gayle. She stood smiling, giving nothing away,

"Well I assume you are done now," I said firmly and Myron gave a short bow and nodded.

"Of course." He glanced at Gayle and nodded before turning on his heel and heading to a black sports car sitting a little way off.

I watched as he got in the car and the car drove off down the road out of the coven.

"I don't like him," Charlene said as she came to stand up next to me. "There is something very dark about him." I didn't say anything but I couldn't agree more.

Chapter 5

Andriana

A THICK CLOUD OF unease hung over me as I tried to put Myron's unnerving visit out of my mind. The scent of burning sage heavy in the air, I moved through the coven house, tidying up and busying myself with mundane tasks. As Priestess of the Lake Key Coven, I had a responsibility to keep my life in order, even when it felt like chaos was lurking just around the corner.

"Hey, Andriana," Gayle called from the living room, her voice startling me out of my thoughts. She stood there, an uncertain smile on her face as she shifted her weight from one foot to the other. "I've been thinking... I'm going to pack up my things and head home."

"Home?" I echoed, trying to mask my surprise. I couldn't deny that Gayle could be annoying at times, but we had a history together. We'd studied magic side by side, and her support had always meant so much to me.

"Yeah, I just feel like its time for me to move on, you know? Things have been so intense lately." Her blue eyes met mine, searching for understanding. I forced a smile, nodding.

"Of course, Gayle. If that's what you think is best." A flicker of relief crossed her face, and I felt a pang of guilt for secretly being grateful she wouldn't be sticking around. We both needed space to grow, and maybe this was for the best.

"Thank you, Andriana. You're the best." She stepped forward, wrapping her arms around me in a tight embrace. I hugged her back, breathing in the familiar scent of lavender that clung to her.

"Take care and don't hesitate to reach out if you need anything. You're always welcome here," I whispered, feeling the weight of our shared memories pressing down on me.

"Same goes for you, Andriana. I'll miss this place." She pulled away, her eyes glistening with unshed tears. "Well, I better get packing."

"Good luck, Gayle," I called after her as she disappeared down the hallway. A heavy silence settled over the house as I stood there, contemplating where life would take us both from here.

With determination, I threw myself back into my duties, tending to the herbs in the garden and sorting through old spell books. Despite my best efforts, thoughts of Myron and his ominous prophecy kept creeping back in, casting a dark shadow over my day. A week had passed, and I found myself kneeling in the soft earth of my herb garden, tending to the delicate plants with practised hands. The scent of rosemary and sage filled the air as I pruned and harvested, but despite the soothing atmosphere, I couldn't shake the lingering shadow of Myron's words.

"Focus, Andriana," I muttered to myself, brushing the soil from my palms. "You've got plenty of other things to worry about."

As if on cue, the phone rang, its shrill sound slicing through the peaceful afternoon. I sighed, pushing myself to my feet and brushing off my knees before hurrying inside to answer it.

"Hello?" I said, my voice slightly breathless.

"Andriana? It's Mirriam Willowvane. Is Gayle there?"

"Mirriam?" Confusion knit my brow as I leaned against the kitchen counter. "No, she left a week ago. She said she was going home."

"Really?" Mirriam's dismissive tone grated on my nerves. "Well, she hasn't shown up here. Probably off on some childish adventure, as usual." My stomach churned with unease at her lack of concern for her own daughter.

"I'll ask around, see if anyone's heard from her."

"Thanks, dear." The line went dead, leaving me with a sinking feeling in my gut. Without hesitation, I grabbed my cell phone and dialled Charlene's number.

"Charlene, it's Andriana. Can you come over? Something's happened with Gayle, and I need your help."

"Of course," she replied, her voice steady and reassuring. "I'll be right there."

As I waited for Charlene, I paced the living room, my thoughts racing. With the tension between witches and werewolves, reaching out to Becca wasn't an easy decision, but I needed her help. I took a deep breath and dialled the familiar number.

"Becca," I said, my voice shaking slightly as I heard her familiar laughter on the other end of the line. "Have you seen Gayle recently? She was supposed to return to Mirriam's place last week, but she never made it there."

"Gayle?" Becca chuckled, her warm voice wrapping around me like a comforting hug. "No way she'd voluntarily go near a werewolf pack, Andriana. But if you're worried, I'll help you find her."

"Thank you," I whispered, relief flooding through me at the offer. "I have a really bad feeling about this."

"Stay put," Becca ordered gently. "Trenton and I will come to you. We'll figure this out together."

"Thanks, Becca." My gratitude was genuine, and I found myself tearing up as I hung up the phone. Our friendship had survived even the most challenging of circumstances, and I knew I could rely on her now.

Charlene arrived just as I finished brewing a pot of tea, her serene presence calming me instantly. As we sat in the living room, sipping our tea in silence, I couldn't help but feel that something monumental was about to happen, a pivotal moment where the pieces of my life would click into place. We settled into the living room to wait for Becca and Trenton, the scent of jasmine tea wafting through the air as we sipped from our cups in silence. The grandfather clock in the corner ticked away the minutes, each beat echoing in my chest like a drumbeat leading to battle.

"Becca and Trenton must be close by now," Charlene noted, worry creasing her brow. "You know they'll do everything they can to help us find Gayle."

"I know," I agreed, my fingers twisting in my lap. "I just can't shake this feeling that something... significant is about to happen."

"Trust your intuition, Andriana," Charlene counselled softly. "You've always had a gift for sensing when things are coming together."

"Maybe you're right," I mused, staring out the window as the sun dipped below the horizon, painting the sky in shades of red and purple. "I just hope we find her soon."

"Have faith, Andriana." Charlene reached over and squeezed my hand, offering reassurance with her gentle touch.

Time seemed to slow as I paced the living room, my agitation growing with each passing minute. The air felt heavy, thick with anticipation and the weight of the unknown. My mother's words echoed in my mind, her voice a distant whisper from the past:

"Andriana, you have a gift for sensing when the pieces of life's puzzle will connect and change everything." I could never quite fathom what she meant, but now, it resonated within me, reverberating through my very core. My heart raced, a steady thrum against my ribcage, urging me to prepare for whatever was to come.

"Try to relax, Andriana," Charlene murmured, her voice a balm against the storm of thoughts ravaging my mind. "We'll figure this out together."

"Relax?" I scoffed, struggling to find solace in her reassurances. "How can I? Gayle is missing, and I feel like something big is about to happen."

"Perhaps that's because it is," she replied cryptically, her gaze fixed on some distant point.

A sudden, forceful knock at the door shattered the tense silence, and I jumped, my heart leaping into my throat. Charlene arched an eyebrow, a wry smile tugging at the corner of her mouth.

"Seems they've arrived," she said, gesturing toward the door.

"Right."

Taking a deep breath, I strode over to the door and flung it open, my eyes widening at the sight before me. Becca stood on the doorstep, her blue eyes twinkling with warmth and familiarity. Beside her were two men - one with dark blond hair and kind eyes, his frame large but not quite as imposing as the man next to him. This other man had dark hair, strong features, and the most captivating green eyes I'd ever seen. A shiver of attraction snaked down my spine, and I struggled to keep my composure.

"Becca!" I cried, pulling her into a tight embrace. "It's so good to see you."

"Allow me to introduce..." Becca began, but the dark-haired man with vivid green eyes interrupted her with a growl. He shoved her aside and strode into the house.

"Mate," he uttered, his voice resonating with an intensity that sent shivers down my spine.

Without warning, he scooped me up, pressing my back against the hallway wall as he buried his face in the crook of my neck. I gasped at the sudden contact, instinctively wrapping my legs around his waist and my arms around his broad shoulders. His scent, a mixture of earth and pine, intoxicated me as I breathed it in, feeling a magnetic pull between us. His power radiated from his body, seeking mine, intertwining and connecting in ways I had never experienced before. It was then that I understood the puzzle pieces of life clicking into place, just as my mother had always said they would. Our lips met in a fierce, passionate kiss, our surroundings forgotten as we lost ourselves in each other's embrace.

A deep chuckle pulled me from my passion-fuelled haze, and I looked up to see Becca and the other man grinning at us, amusement dancing in their eyes. Charlene stood nearby, a puzzled expression on her face as she tried to understand what was happening. I gently pushed against the man, who reluctantly released me, allowing my feet to touch the ground once more. My cheeks flushed with embarrassment as I realised how brazenly I had acted in front of my friends.

"Ahem," Becca cleared her throat, still smirking. "As I was saying, this is my mate Trenton." She gestured to the blond-haired man, who nodded kindly. "And this... rather enthusiastic gentleman is Alpha Nathaniel Hallows."

"Nice to meet you, Andriana," Nathaniel murmured sheepishly, his eyes flicking to mine before quickly looking away.

"Likewise," I replied, trying to regain my composure. Trenton whispered something in Becca's ear, causing them both to laugh, their love for each other evident in the way they interacted.

"Uh, I'm sorry about that," Nathaniel stammered, his voice rough and resonant. "I didn't believe the mate bond could be so powerful."

"Neither did I," I admitted, unable to hide the blush creeping up my cheeks. The air between us felt charged, electric. It was as if we were two magnets, drawn together by a force beyond our control.

"Let's all have some tea, shall we?" I suggested, eager to break the tension. "We can discuss our plan in the living room."

"Tea sounds lovely," Becca agreed, her eyes twinkling with amusement. Charlene nodded, still looking slightly bewildered by the whole situation. As we made our way into the living room, I could feel Nathaniel's gaze on me, like a physical touch that sent shivers down my spine. I fought the urge to look back at him, focusing instead on pouring the tea into delicate china cups. The scent of chamomile filled the air, soothing my frayed nerves.

"Here you go," I said, handing a cup to Becca. She took it with a grateful smile before passing one to her mate, Trenton. Charlene accepted hers with a nod, and finally, I handed a cup to Nathaniel.

"Thank you," he murmured, his fingers brushing against mine as he took the cup. The brief contact sent sparks dancing across my skin, making my heart race. I quickly withdrew my hand, trying to ignore the heat pooling in the pit of my stomach.

"Alright," I began, taking a deep breath to steady myself. "Now that we're all here, let's talk about what we need to do to find Gayle."

"Of course," Becca agreed, setting her cup down on the table. "Charlene mentioned you've already tried a few spells?"

"Yes," I replied, glancing at Charlene. "But we haven't had much luck."

"Then we'll try something else," Becca said determinedly. "I have a few ideas that might help."

"Alright," I said, forcing my voice to remain steady as I placed the teapot back on the table. "Let's get down to business." I took a deep breath and began recounting the events of the past week.

"Gayle, Charlene and I helped the Alpha and Luna of the Silver Stone pack with their recent troubles. After that, we had an unexpected visit from Myron, a sorcerer who seemed to know about a prophecy involving me."

"Prophecy?" Becca asked, her eyes widening in surprise. I nodded.

"He didn't give much information, just that he wanted me to join him. I refused, of course." My hands tightened around the cup, the ceramic creaking under my grip.

"But now, Gayle has gone missing. Her mom called today, saying she never made it home."

"Did this Myron mention anything about Gayle?" Trenton asked, his brow furrowed in concern.

"No, but I can't help feeling like it's all connected somehow," I admitted, staring into the dark liquid in my cup as if the answers might reveal themselves there. Trenton leaned forward, resting his elbows on his knees.

"On our way here, I made some calls. A local sorcerer's been asking around about you, Andriana. No one knew his name, but it sounds like it could be this Myron."

"Is he behind Gayle's disappearance, then?" Charlene wondered aloud, worry etched on her face.

"I don't know," I confessed, shaking my head. "But something feels off, and I can't shake the feeling that we're running out of time."

"Then we need to act fast," Nathaniel said, his voice low and determined. I looked at him, momentarily caught in the emerald depths of his eyes.

"Right," I agreed, tearing my gaze away. "We should focus on finding Gayle first. We can deal with Myron and his prophecy later."

"Agreed," Becca said, her demeanour all business now. "Let's put our heads together and figure out our next move."

As we dived into strategizing and planning, I couldn't help but feel a small spark of hope amidst the uncertainty.

"Let's try a location spell," Becca suggested, her blue eyes filled with determination. "It might help us find Gayle."

"Good idea," I agreed, rising from my seat. I hurried upstairs to the room where Gayle had been staying, searching for something that could hold a trace of her essence. My hands grabbed a pillowcase she'd used, and I clutched it tightly as I returned to the others.

"Will this work?" I asked, holding out the pillowcase. Becca took it from me, inspecting it closely before nodding.

"It should be enough."

We cleared a space in the living room, pushing aside furniture to create an open circle on the floor. Becca, Charlene, and I sat down, legs crossed, forming a tight triangle. The pillowcase lay in the centre, its pale fabric glowing faintly in the dim light.

"Focus your energy on Gayle," Becca instructed, her voice soft yet commanding. "Envision her face, her voice, her presence. We need to connect with her essence through our combined power." I closed my eyes and concentrated, calling forth memories of Gayle, her laughter, her kindness, her unwavering loyalty. As our energies melded together, I felt a surge of warmth pulsating through me, like a beacon of light guiding us toward her. Becca chanted her Latin, her voice steady and strong. The air around us hummed with power, and the scent of lilacs, Gayle's favourite flower, filled the room. A shimmering image appeared above the pillowcase, wavering like a mirage before solidifying into a clear picture: a dark, abandoned warehouse by the edge of town.

"Is that...?" Charlene trailed off, her eyes widening in recognition.

"Looks like it," Trenton confirmed grimly. "We'd been investigating that location for other reasons, but I didn't expect to find her there."

Before we could delve into planning our next move, the shrill ring of the house phone pierced the charged atmosphere. My heart leaped into my throat as I scrambled to pick it up, my hands shaking with nerves.

"Hello?" I answered hesitantly, my voice barely above a whisper.

"Ah, Andriana," came a silky voice from the other end, a voice I recognised all too well. Myron. "I felt your power again. I assume you're finally ready to talk about working with me?"

Chapter 6

Andriana

"Please, Myron," I begged into the phone, my voice shaking with urgency, "let Gayle go. You don't need her." On the other end of the line, Myron's sinister laugh sent shivers down my spine.

"Oh, Andriana," he purred, his voice dripping with malice, "I have no intention of letting my new little toy go, unless you're willing to take her place." My heart pounded in my chest as I gripped the phone tighter, trying to control my fear and anger. I knew I had to be careful with my words; one wrong move could spell disaster for Gayle.

"Fine," I said, my voice barely a whisper. "What do you want me to do?"

"Meet me at the abandoned warehouse on the edge of the city on Kayson Street in two hours," Myron instructed, his tone firm and cold. "Come alone. No other witches and definitely no wolves. If you don't follow my instructions, Gayle will pay painfully for it."

"Okay," I choked out before the line went dead, leaving me with nothing but the deafening silence of the room.

The cold receiver slipped from my trembling fingers, the dial tone echoing like a death knell in the silence that followed. My heart hammered wildly in my chest, threatening to burst as the gravity of the situation settled over me like a suffocating shroud. I could barely breathe, let alone think, but I knew one thing for certain, my dear friend Gayle was in grave danger, and it was all because of me.

"Andriana?" Nathaniel's voice cut through the haze of fear and guilt, his strong arms wrapping around me as if he could protect me from the storm raging inside. The warmth of our mate bond pulsed between us, a soothing balm to my frayed nerves.

"What did he say? Are you alright?"

I looked up into Nathaniel's concerned green eyes, seeing the same fierce determination and unwavering loyalty that had drawn me to him in the first place. I couldn't keep this from him, nor could I bear to face the others alone. Taking a shuddering breath, I whispered the horrifying truth.

"Myron has Gayle. He wants to trade her for me."

"Absolutely not!" Nathaniel growled, his eyes flashing with anger at the very thought. "I just found you, Andriana. I won't lose you now, especially not to that monster."

"Please, Nathaniel," I begged, gripping his arms tightly as tears threatened to spill down my cheeks. "Gayle is my friend, my sister in magic. I can't let her suffer because of me. I have to go." Our gazes locked, a silent battle of wills as we each struggled to put our own fears aside for the sake of someone we loved.

"Are you mad?" Trenton exclaimed, his blue eyes wide with disbelief. "You can't go alone, Andriana. It's too dangerous."

"Exactly," Nathaniel chimed in, his voice firm and unwavering. "I won't let you face Myron by yourself. I don't care what he said about coming alone, we'll find a way to help without him knowing." I glared at them both, my determination fuelled by the fear for Gayle's safety.

"If you think you can order me around so easily, then you've found the wrong bloody mate, Nathaniel," I snapped, my temper flaring as I faced him down. Nathaniel's eyes widened in surprise but were soon replaced with a hint of admiration. He was quickly learning just how stubborn I could be, and it seemed that my fierce spirit only made him love me more.

"Fine," he conceded, his jaw clenched in frustration. "But if I have to lock you in my car to keep you safe, I will."

"Alright," I sighed, knowing that I had other ways to win this battle.

As the others murmured their agreement, Trenton pulled out his phone and dialled their pack Beta, Marshall Hayes, to prepare their warriors for the fight ahead. The tension in the air was palpable, a heavy weight pressing down on us all as we silently acknowledged the gravity of the situation.

"Marshall, we're going to need every available warrior," Trenton spoke quietly and urgently into the phone. "Myron has taken one of our own, and we need to get her back." I paced nervously, my thoughts a chaotic whirlwind of fear and anger. I couldn't believe that Myron had managed to manipulate me so easily, drawing me into his twisted game like a moth to a flame. But there was no turning back now, I had to face him head-on and pray that I could outsmart him for Gayle's sake.

"Alright, listen closely," I told Nathaniel and the others, my voice barely more than a whisper. "The warehouse we're going to is on the other side of town, just beyond the new shopping centre. Be prepared for anything." With that said, I climbed into my car and drove off, leaving them behind to coordinate their plan. As I navigated the dark streets, my thoughts were consumed with guilt and fear. I wished I had never involved Gayle in this mess, she didn't deserve any of it. Though I was grateful for the support of the Half Moon pack and some of my best witches from the Lake Key coven, I couldn't shake the feeling that Myron would somehow find out about our plan and do something terrible to Gayle as retribution.

"Please, Gayle," I murmured under my breath, gripping the steering wheel tightly. "Hold on, just a little longer."

Ten minutes away from the warehouse, I pulled over to the side of the road and waited. My heart hammered against my ribcage as the black SUV I had been expecting finally appeared in my rearview mirror. It came to a stop behind me, and Nathaniel's tall figure emerged from the driver's seat. He approached my car, his eyes locked on mine as he leaned down to the open window. Without saying a word, he pressed a quick, tender kiss to my lips, sending a jolt of warmth through my entire body.

"Don't worry, Andriana," he reassured me, his voice low and steady. "The plan is set. We'll be watching your back every step of the way. But if you find yourself in danger at any point." he paused, his gaze intense, "I won't hesitate to go in all guns or claws blazing."

"Thank you, Nathaniel," I whispered, my throat tight with emotion.

"Remember," he added, "we're in this together. We'll find Gayle and put an end to Myron's twisted games." With a final lingering look, Nathaniel returned to his SUV, which sped off into the night as I sat there, trying to calm my racing heart.

The engine roared to life as I pressed down on the accelerator, my hands gripping the wheel tightly. My stomach churned with a mixture of fear and determination, like an alchemist's potion brewing inside me. I knew I had promised Nathaniel that I would be safe, but the thought of Gayle in danger was too much to bear. I could only hope that whatever happened, my friends and Nathaniel would forgive me.

As I pulled up outside the warehouse on Kayson Street, I knew full well that the area around me would be deserted. The moon cast eerie shadows across the dark, crumbling buildings, making it feel like the very air held secrets. A pressure of dark energy was already palpable, a sinister presence lurking in the corner of the building. It sent shivers down my spine, but I knew that it was where I would find Myron.

The cold wind whipped my hair across my face as I stepped out of the car, goosebumps prickling my skin. The desolation of the area hung heavy, pressing down upon me like a suffocating weight. I swallowed hard, trying to steady my racing heart.

"You can do this, Andriana," I whispered to myself, hoping that somehow, saying it aloud would make it more real. I scanned the empty grounds, taking in the eerie silhouette of the warehouse against the backdrop of an ink-black sky. The door stood wide open, its yawning mouth seeming to taunt me with its easy accessibility. It was as if Myron wanted me to know just how foolish I was being, walking straight into his trap.

As I approached the entrance, tendrils of dark energy snaked towards me, their blackness at odds with the natural shadows that surrounded them. An icy shiver ran down my spine as I realised that not only was Myron aware of my arrival, but he was also trying to ensnare me in his twisted web. The tendrils reached for me, drawn to the power that coursed through my veins, yearning to corrupt it.

"Get away from me!" I hissed, swiping at the tendrils with my hand. They recoiled and dissipated, only to reappear moments later, more persistent than before. There was something almost seductive about their dance, a morbid allure that threatened to consume me if I let my guard down. But no matter how enticing they were, I couldn't afford to lose control - not when Gayle's life hung in the balance.

"Enough!" I shouted, channelling my anger into a burst of energy that sent the tendrils spiralling away from me. As they retreated, I felt a small surge of triumph, but it was short-lived. I knew that the real battle had yet to begin. Taking a deep breath, I steeled myself for what lay ahead. I could feel the darkness lurking just beyond the warehouse entrance, waiting like a hungry predator to claim me as its prey. But I refused to be devoured without a fight. For Gayle, for my friends, and for Nathaniel, I would stand my ground against Myron and whatever twisted games he had in store for me.

I followed the tendrils through the dark, oppressive corridors of the abandoned warehouse, my heart pounding in my chest. The suffocating darkness seemed to close in on me with every step I took. Shadows danced along the walls, mocking my fear and determination. My senses were heightened, alert to any sign of danger or deceit. Finally, I found myself in front of a large, heavy metal door. The door was lit up with a mass of black pulsing tendrils snaking out of it, their movements hypnotic and otherworldly. I knew that behind this door lay the answers I sought and the fate of my dear friend Gayle. With trembling hands, I grasped the cold metal handle and struggled to pull the massive door open. It groaned in protest, as if it had been undisturbed for decades. The air inside the room was heavy, tainted with an unsettling aura that sent shivers down my spine. Steeling myself, I stepped into the dimly lit chamber.

The sight that greeted me was enough to make bile rise in my throat. On a thin, dirty mattress, Gayle knelt, her once vibrant blond hair now matted with dirt and sweat. Her face was bloodied and bruised, her clothes torn and hanging off her slender frame. Chains bound her wrists, attaching her to the wall like a prisoner. But what truly horrified me was the expression on her face, she looked almost happy, yet her eyes were vacant, devoid of any recognition or emotion. As her gaze fixed on the shadowed figure across the room, it was as if she were praying to it.

"Gayle," I choked out, my voice barely above a whisper. "What has he done to you?"

My heart caught in my throat as the figure turned toward me, his face illuminated by the dim light filtering through the door. Myron's vivid blue eyes met mine, and a sinister smile crept across his lips.

"Ah, Andriana, my dear. Thank you for coming. I trust you followed all my instructions?" His voice oozed with oily charm, sending shivers down my spine. I nodded, regretting what I had done already.

"Yes," I replied, knowing that I was telling the truth and that somewhere across the city, Nathaniel and the others were heading to a fake location.

Chapter 7

Andriana

My heart pounded in my chest as I faced off against Myron. His black hair fell across his forehead, framing his vivid blue eyes that were filled with cruel intent.

"Let Gayle go," I demanded, my voice echoing through the vast space. I had sent Nathaniel and my friends to the wrong address intentionally, hoping to protect them from this confrontation. But now, I was alone without hope for help. Myron smirked, raising a hand to send an energy blast towards me. I quickly threw up a defensive shield around myself, deflecting his attack. The force of the impact rattled my shield, but it held strong. I gritted my teeth and tried to push past him to get to Gayle, who was bound in chains on the other side of the room.

"Leave her alone," I said, my voice wavering despite my best efforts. "I've come as you asked. Now let her go." Myron turned to Gayle, his lips curled into a smug smile.

"Do you want to leave me?" he asked her.

"Please, don't let me go!" Gayle cried out, tears streaming down her cheeks. Her blond hair stuck to her face and her blue eyes were filled with utter desperation. My heart clenched at the sight of her so broken.

"See?" Myron said, turning back to me. "She doesn't want to go." Realisation dawned on me, Myron had cast some sort of compulsion spell on Gayle. My anger flared, and I clenched my fists.

"Remove the spell, now!" I demanded.

"Sorry, love" he said, his voice dripping with malice. "I've no intention of doing that until I have some assurance that you won't try to escape." I knew that he wasn't going to make this easy. My mind raced as I tried to figure out a way to break the compulsion spell without putting Gayle in further danger.

"What do you want? Just let her go. I am here like you asked."

"Maybe," he said, drawing out the word as if savouring my desperation. "But if you think I'll just let you walk away, you're sorely mistaken."

"I won't leave," I said, looking directly into Myron's cold blue eyes. "My word is my bond." Myron laughed, a cruel sound that echoed off the warehouse walls.

"Your word? The same word you gave to your friends when you sent them on a wild goose chase? Forgive me if I don't put much stock in that." His words stung, but I refused to let him see how much they affected me. Instead, I stood tall and defiant, ready for whatever he had in store.

"Fine," I spat. "What do you want?"

"Something far more binding," Myron replied with a wicked smile. "A blood bond. A ritual connecting our souls for lifetimes to come." I felt my stomach twist at the thought. Blood bonds were not to be taken lightly. They bound two people together in ways that could never be undone, unbreakable connections that transcended time and space. To form such a bond with Myron would be a fate worse than death.

"Never," I whispered, my voice shaking with suppressed fury. "I won't do it."

"Then Gayle remains mine," he said simply, turning back to look at her as if she were a prize possession. My heart ached at the sight of her trembling and sobbing under Myron's control. I couldn't bear the thought of leaving her like this, that was completely out of the question. Yet the idea of being forever bound to Myron was a nightmare I couldn't endure.

"Please," I begged, tears pricking at the corners of my eyes. "There has to be another way. Anything else."

"Nothing else will suffice," Myron said, his voice cold and unyielding. "It's the blood bond or nothing. Your choice." As I stood there, torn between my love for Gayle and my own self-preservation, I realised just how trapped I truly was. Myron had crafted this situation perfectly, ensuring that whatever choice I made, I would lose something precious. I hated him more than anyone in that moment.

"Absolutely not," I spat, the words filled with venom. "I refuse to do such a ritual, Myron. I'll find another way to free Gayle."

"Ah, so you think you can just take her by force?" he mocked, his laughter echoing around the dimly lit warehouse. "Do you truly believe you're powerful enough, Andriana?" His sneering tone ate away at my resolve, and doubt crept into my mind like a poisonous vine. I stared back at him, my blue eyes meeting his piercing gaze, attempting to convey a confidence I didn't feel.

"Maybe I am," I said, my voice wavering ever so slightly. Myron's grin widened as he took in the uncertainty on my face. He knew he had me cornered, and it only served to fuel his arrogance further.

"Even if you could overpower me," he continued, his voice a low growl, "it wouldn't make a difference. The moment you take Gayle from me, the compulsion spell will have her running straight back to my arms. And she'll be all too eager to accept whatever punishment I choose to inflict upon her for your actions."

My heart pounded in my chest as I stared into Myron's vivid blue eyes, his smirk only fueling the anger that burned within me. I needed to know more about this prophecy he was so obsessed with, and why it involved me.

"Seriously, Myron," I demanded, struggling to keep my voice steady. "Why are you so intent on this prophecy? Why am I a part of your twisted plans?" He leaned back against the cold, damp wall, his grin never fading.

"The child of the prophecy, Andriana, will change the world. They will be the beginning of a new, powerful species. The fate of the world will depend on how the child chooses their path. Can't you see? I'm eager to shape the child's choice in my favour." I shuddered at the thought of what he might do to manipulate an innocent life.

"And just what do you mean by that?" I asked, unable to hide the disgust that laced my words. Myron pushed off the wall and took a step closer, his eyes locked on mine.

"I will ensure that the child is raised under my influence, moulded by my guidance. It's up to you, Andriana, if you want to be a part of that great new future or not. But rest assured, I will have the child, regardless."

The fire inside me burned hotter than the rage coursing through my veins, and I knew I couldn't let Myron corrupt my future child. This was about more than just us; it was about the fate of an entire world that hung in the balance. I refused to be the reason the scales tipped in his favour. I screamed, my voice cracking as I released all the pent-up anger within me. A surge of energy erupted from my hands, taking the form of a brilliant, blinding light that collided with Myron's chest. The force of the blast sent him flying across the room, smacking against the far wall with a sickening crunch.

"Gayle!" I called out, hoping against hope that she'd hear my voice and fight against Myron's control. I sprinted towards her, feeling the rush of adrenaline fuelling my every step. As I reached her side, I chanted a quick spell to shatter the chains that bound her. They fell away with a clatter, leaving the cold, damp floor beneath them.

"Come on, we need to go," I urged, pulling Gayle to her feet with as much strength as my trembling limbs could muster. But instead of following me, Gayle began to scream and thrash in my grasp, her eyes wild with fear.

"Leave me alone! You can't take me from my master!" she shrieked, her voice hoarse from the exertion. I felt my heart break at the sight of my once-strong friend reduced to this pitiful state, so utterly lost and under Myron's control.

"Gayle, please," I begged, tears pricking at the corners of my eyes. "You are stronger than this. Don't let him win." She continued to struggle against me, her nails digging into my arms as if she were trying to anchor herself to this dark place. I could see the internal battle raging behind her eyes, the brief flicker of recognition that threatened to break through.

"Gayle, fight it," I whispered, searching for any hint of the woman who'd once been like a sister to me. "Please, don't let him destroy you."

My heart raced as I struggled to hold on to Gayle, her screams echoing through the abandoned warehouse. But then I heard it, a sinister chuckle from the other side of the room.

"Did you really think it would be so easy?" Myron's voice seemed to slither through the shadows, his vivid blue eyes gleaming with malicious intent as he hauled himself up from where my energy blast had thrown him. The smug grin on his face made my blood boil.

"Go fuck yourself," I spat, casting a quick subdue spell on Gayle. Her body went limp in my arms, her struggles ceasing immediately.

"Such language, Andriana," he drawled, his amusement only fuelling my anger. "But you know, you've barely begun to understand what you're truly up against." As I tried to guide Gayle out of the room, Myron recited something that stopped me dead in my tracks.

"In the world where shadows blend with light,
A maiden of twenty-five shall rise from the night.
Descendant of Diana, Queen of Witches and Beasts,
Half witch, half wolf, her lineage in the least."

His laughter echoed through the room, chilling me to the bone.

"Tell me, Andriana, have you had any interesting encounters with new wolves lately?" My mind raced, thoughts of Nathaniel invading my consciousness. The prophecy rang in my ears, its implications setting my nerves on fire. How could he know? The words felt like an icy dagger carving into my soul, and I knew I couldn't ignore their significance.

"Leave him out of this," I growled, gripping Gayle's arm tighter.

"Ah, so you have met someone," Myron said, his voice dripping with satisfaction. "Well, I'm sure he'll make a fine addition to our little family once we've completed our ritual."

My heart pounded in my chest as Myron's words echoed through my mind, intertwining with memories of Nathaniel and our encounters. I knew I had to ignore him; he was just trying to manipulate me. But the prophecy, if it had anything to do with my child, I needed to know.

"Tell me the rest," I demanded, my voice trembling with a mixture of fear and determination. "I need to know." Myron chuckled darkly, pushing himself off the wall and standing tall before me.

"Oh, Andriana, you are so eager for knowledge. Very well, I'll tell you everything you want to know... after we complete the blood bond ritual." He smirked, clearly enjoying the power he held over me.

"Go to hell," I spat, my anger flaring up once more. Myron's voice dripped with mockery as he spoke.

"Without the knowledge of the prophecy and my help, you'll be condemning your child to a life of being hunted by anyone who wants that power for themselves." I froze, clenching my fists at my sides, trying to keep my composure.

"Make no mistake," he continued, his voice low and menacing. "I will dedicate my life to hunting down your child until she is in my hands, for me to shape as I see fit. And not only will I hunt you both down, but as soon as dear Gayle returns to me, and she will, I'll ensure she dies in the most public and painful way imaginable. Everyone will know it was your fault."

My heart pounded in my chest, each beat echoing the terror and despair that coursed through me. The grim reality of the situation closed in around me, suffocating any hope I had of escaping this nightmare unscathed. I knew Myron would stop at nothing to achieve his twisted goals, and the thought of my friends suffering because of my actions was unbearable.

"Fine," I whispered, desperately clinging to the belief that there must be a way out of this. "I'll do the blood bond ritual. But I swear to you, Myron, if you harm Gayle or anyone else I care about, I will find a way to break this bond and end you."

"Ah, such conviction!" Myron exclaimed, clapping his hands together in mock delight. "That's what I like to hear. Let's begin, shall we?" His dark eyes locked onto mine, and I felt the weight of the decision I had just made. I swallowed hard, steeling myself for what was to come. There was no turning back now.

In a flourish, Myron snapped his fingers, and the room erupted in flickering candlelight. The once-veiled walls revealed themselves to be adorned with sigils and ancient symbols, their meaning beyond my understanding. I couldn't help but shudder at the thought of what other dark secrets this place held.

"Shall we?" Myron gestured toward a pair of chairs tucked into a previously darkened corner. I glanced at Gayle, who lay motionless on the mattress. With a heavy heart, I left her there and followed Myron, the sickening feeling in my stomach growing stronger as I approached the chairs. As I sat down opposite him, Myron began chanting in an unfamiliar language. The air around us felt charged, and black tendrils started to materialise out of thin air, wrapping themselves around my arms like serpents. I resisted the urge to recoil; I had to see this through for the sake of my child and Gayle. Myron's hand clenched a silver dagger, blood dripping from the fresh cut he'd made. He passed it to me expectantly, and without a moment's hesitation, I sliced into my own palm. Blood welled up, and the tendrils eagerly pushed their way through the wound and into my bloodstream. The darkness invaded my body, suffocating and relentless. I fought to steady my breathing as the tendrils inched closer and closer to my heart, the point of no return. I couldn't bear to think about being bound to Myron in this life and the next, but what choice did I have?

"Embrace it, Andriana," Myron taunted, his smile wicked and triumphant. "Soon, you'll be mine." I knew that once this ritual was complete, I would be bound to him, and his death would mean mine as well. But I couldn't give up; I had to find a way to protect my child and break free from Myron's grasp. As the tendrils neared my heart, the pain intensified, and I felt a crushing weight on my chest. I wanted nothing more than to tear myself away from the ritual, but I forced myself to remain still, determined to see it through for those I loved.

Something snapped my attention away from the ritual. There was something happening in the hallway outside. The moment the crashing sound filled the room, I felt a surge of hope and terror. A large black wolf burst through the doorway, the metal door slamming against the wall with a deafening clang. His gold eyes blazed with fury, and as he scanned the room, our eyes locked. In that instant, I knew it was Nathaniel. The knowledge gave me the strength I needed to rip myself away from the ritual. Channelling my anger and desperation, I sent a light blast towards Myron. The force knocked both of us into opposite walls, and pain seared through my body as I collided with the cold, unforgiving surface. I cried out, my breath stolen by the impact. Nathaniel snarled at Myron, lunging for him with fangs bared. But before he could reach the sinister sorcerer, Gayle let out a guttural scream and leaped in front of Myron, shielding him from Nathaniel's attack.

"Stop!" I screamed, my heart pounding in my chest. Nathaniel twisted mid-air, narrowly avoiding tearing Gayle's throat open. Instead, he crashed into another wall, his massive frame shaking the entire room.

I ignored the pain coursing through my body and scrambled to Nathaniel's side. The moment my hand touched his fur, he shifted back into his human form, panting from the exertion of his transformation.

"Are you alright?" I asked worriedly, my voice trembling.

"Never better," Nathaniel gasped, his golden eyes filled with determination. As if summoned by our exchange, the room suddenly filled with familiar faces. Trenton, Becca, and others rushed in, their expressions a mix of relief and concern.

"Where the bloody hell is the sorcerer?" Trenton demanded, scanning the room with narrowed eyes. We all looked around, but Myron had vanished, leaving only the sobbing Gayle clinging to the wall where he had been moments before.

"Damn it," I muttered, my fingers curling into tight fists. "He's gone."

Chapter 8

Andriana

I COULD FEEL THE anger boiling within me as I searched the room for Myron. I gritted my teeth and clenched my fists, my magical energy pulsing around me like a storm.

"I have to go after him, Nathaniel," I insisted, muscles tensing for action. "He can't be allowed to just vanish like that."

"Rest, Andriana," Nathaniel ordered, his deep voice tinged with concern. He placed a hand on my shoulder, attempting to ground me. "You're not in any condition to chase after anyone right now."

"Damn it, you don't understand!" I snapped, shrugging off his touch. "We need to know if Myron is a danger or not." My thoughts raced along with my pounding heart, images of what he might do next flooding my mind. Nathaniel's eyes softened as he gazed at me, but his expression remained firm.

"Listen to me," he said, his voice low and commanding. "We will find Myron, and we will deal with him. But right now, your main concern should be getting your friend home."

His words pierced through the fog of my worry, drawing my attention to Gayle. She was sobbing, her entire body trembling as she struggled against the iron grip of Trenton and Marshall. Her blue eyes were wild and desperate as she tried to break free from their hold, her focus solely on finding Myron.

"Please, let me go!" Gayle wailed, tears streaming down her face. "I have to find him!" Seeing her so distraught broke something inside me, and my resolve hardened. Nathaniel was right; I needed to focus on helping her. Taking a deep breath, I forced myself to calm down and approached my tormented friend.

"Gayle," I whispered gently, placing a hand on her arm. "We'll get through this, I promise."

"Find Myron..." she choked out between sobs, her gaze pleading with me.

"We will," I assured her, anything to placate her, my heart aching for her pain. "But first, let's get you home and safe."

As we moved away from the scene of chaos and into the cold night air, my thoughts turned to Myron and the danger he posed. But for now, I had to shove those worries aside and focus on the friend who needed me most. With every step, Gayle's resistance intensified as Trenton and Marshall struggled to guide her toward the car. Her screams pierced the air, her eyes wild with desperation.

"Let me go!" she shrieked. "I need to find Myron!" My heart clenched in sympathy, but I couldn't let her chase after him. We needed to help her.

"Please, Gayle," I pleaded, my voice cracking. "We're trying to help you."

"Go to hell!" she spat back, her face contorted with rage and betrayal.

The journey back to my home was a harrowing ordeal. As the sky began to lighten with the first hints of dawn, exhaustion weighed heavily on us all. Nathaniel drove in silence, his jaw set in a determined line. Becca, Charlene, Trenton, and Marshall sat quietly, each lost in their thoughts about what had transpired at the warehouse and the challenges that lay ahead. Gayle, however, refused to be silent. She hurled insults and curses at me relentlessly, her voice raw with pain and fury. When we finally arrived at my house, we moved quickly, desperate for the safety it offered. The sun was beginning to rise, casting long shadows across the lawn as we rushed inside.

"Please, Gayle," I said gently as I led her to the guest room. "You need to rest."

"Rest?" she snarled, venom dripping from her words. "What I need is to find Myron, you traitorous bitch!" Her outburst stung, but I tried not to let it show. Instead, I took a deep breath, summoning my strength, and cast another subdue spell. The incantation flowed from my lips like silk, wrapping around her in a gentle embrace.

"Be still, my friend," I whispered as the magic took hold and Gayle's screams finally faded, leaving only ragged breaths and the pounding of my heart in my ears. As she collapsed onto the bed, her body limp with exhaustion, I couldn't shake the feeling that we were all teetering on the edge of disaster. But for now, at least, we were safe.

"Becca, what do you think will happen to Gayle?" I asked, wringing my hands as we all gathered in the living room. My eyes flickered to the stairs leading up to the guest room, an uneasy feeling settling over me.

"From what I can tell," Becca said softly, "the compulsion spell Myron placed on her will only grow stronger the longer she's away from him. We need to find a way to cleanse her system before it consumes her entirely." I nodded, my heart heavy with the weight of responsibility. There was so much at stake, and our time was quickly running out.

"I'll call some witches from the coven," I decided, pulling out my phone. "We'll need their help to perform the cleansing ritual."

As I made the necessary calls, the others tried to process the night's events. Nathaniel sat on the couch, his jaw clenched and his eyes stormy, while Charlene stared blankly at the wall, her gaze unfocused and distant. Trenton and Marshall paced the floor, their nerves frayed and restless. Suddenly, a loud crash echoed through the house, followed by the sound of shattering glass. My heart leaped into my throat as I raced towards the stairs, dread coiling in my stomach. The others were close behind, their expressions mirroring my own fear. When we reached the guest room, the sight that greeted us was chilling. Gayle stood near the broken window, shards of glass littering the floor around her, her eyes wild and desperate as she attempted to climb out.

"Gayle, no!" I cried, lunging forward to grab her arm. But it was Nathaniel who managed to pull her back, his strong arms wrapping around her waist as he hauled her onto the bed.

"Let me go!" she screamed, thrashing violently in his grip. "I need to find Myron!"

"Gayle, please," I pleaded, tears prickling my eyes. "We're trying to help you."

"Help me?" she spat, her blue eyes blazing with fury. "You're keeping me from him! You're killing me!"

As I stared at her distraught face, I knew that we couldn't risk leaving her unrestrained any longer. Turning to Nathaniel, I said,

"We need to clean out the basement. It's the only place we can keep her secure while we wait for the others." Nathaniel nodded grimly, his eyes never leaving Gayle. I only hoped that the witches from my coven would arrive soon, armed with the knowledge and power we desperately needed to save our friend.

"Becca, Trenton, please stay with Gayle," I instructed, my voice wavering slightly. "We'll prepare the basement as quickly as possible."

"Of course, Andriana," Becca replied, her eyes filled with concern and determination. Trenton simply gave a curt nod, his face etched with worry.

As Nathaniel and I descended the stairs to the basement, the air grew heavy with the scent of damp earth and lingering traces of magic. The space was dimly lit, filled with boxes, old furniture, and countless trinkets from my family's past. It was a chaotic mess, but one that held a sense of familiarity and security for me.

"Here," I said, leading Nathaniel to the far end of the room where a heavy metal door stood, its surface marred by scratches and dents. "Behind this door is where I keep anything that needs to be secured – supplies, enchanted objects, you name it." Nathaniel nodded, his brow furrowed with concentration.

"Let's get started then. We don't have much time."

I unlocked the door with a wave of my hand, and we both stepped inside. Shelves lined the walls, laden with jars of herbs, bottles of potions, and an array of mystical artefacts. The very air seemed charged with magical energy, crackling around us like static electricity.

"Help me clear some space," I said, my hands already reaching for a stack of dusty books. "Charlene will take the valuable and dangerous items to her house for safekeeping, while Stephen and Marshall help her transport them."

"Understood," Nathaniel replied, his hands deftly sorting through the various objects. As we worked, I couldn't help but feel the weight of the situation pressing down on me. Time seemed to slip through our fingers like sand, each passing moment another reminder of the danger Gayle faced.

"Will this really hold her?" Nathaniel asked, interrupting my thoughts. "What if she breaks through the door or finds another way out?"

"Trust me," I said, trying to ease his concerns with a reassuring smile. "This room was designed to contain even the most powerful of beings. It will hold."

"Alright," he conceded, his voice laced with doubt. "I just want her, and you, to be safe."

"Me too," I whispered, my heart aching in my chest. "You have no idea how much I want that."

As I wiped the sweat from my brow, I couldn't shake the feeling that something was off between Nathaniel and me. His movements were tense, his jaw clenched, as if he was trying to hold back a torrent of unspoken words.

"Are you alright?" I asked hesitantly, pausing in my task of clearing away the clutter. He looked up from the box he was sorting through, his eyes meeting mine with a flash of irritation.

"I'm fine," he replied in short, brisk tones. I frowned, knowing instinctively that he wasn't being honest with me. It seemed as though the very air around him crackled with tension, his energy radiating anger like a storm cloud about to burst.

"You're bullshitting," I accused, placing my hands on my hips. "I can tell by your energy that you're pissed off." Nathaniel growled low in his throat before finally snapping,

"Of course I'm pissed off, Andriana!" He slammed the box down onto the floor, making me jump. "You lied to me about the location and put yourself in danger. What the hell were you thinking?"

"Me?" I shouted back, my own temper flaring to life. "I did it to protect you, Nathaniel! This involves everyone, including you!"

"Explain," he demanded, his eyes blazing with fury.

"Gayle's condition, Myron's twisted games... they affect us all. Our friends, our families, our communities are all at risk," I explained, my voice shaking with the weight of my emotions. "I had to act, even if it meant risking my own safety."

"Damn it, Andriana!" Nathaniel roared, running a hand through his hair in frustration. "You were being selfish with your actions. I've only just found you, and yet you're taking stupid risks that could take you away from me!"

"Protecting those I care about isn't selfish, Nathaniel," I screamed back, my heart pounding in my chest. "It's what we do as leaders, as witches and werewolves. We fight for our people, even if it means putting ourselves in harm's way."

"Then let me fight with you," he said, his voice a low growl. I stared at him, his words echoing through my mind like a powerful incantation. As much as I wanted to shield him from the darkness that surrounded us, I knew he was right.

"Alright," I said, taking a deep breath as I prepared to reveal the prophecy that had been haunting my thoughts.

"Myron told me about a prophecy that involves both of us. He said, 'In the world where shadows blend with light, A maiden of twenty-five shall rise from the night. Descendant of Diana, Queen of Witches and Beasts, Half witch, half wolf, her lineage in the least.'" Nathaniel's eyes widened, his anger momentarily replaced by surprise.

"That's... that's about you," he whispered, his voice laced with disbelief.

"About us," I corrected him, my heart hammering against my ribs. "Myron knew that we had found each other as fated mates. The prophecy is about our child."

"Are you sure?" he asked, searching my eyes for any hint of doubt.

"I'm certain," I replied, my voice wavering slightly under the weight of the revelation. Nathaniel growled, his anger reigniting like a firestorm. He grabbed hold of me, his strong fingers digging into my arms as he pulled me close.

"If I'm involved in this," he snarled, "then I should be involved in the decision-making as well. You can't keep shutting me out, Andriana."

I tried to speak, but Nathaniel silenced me by slamming me up against the wall. The impact took my breath away, and for a moment, all I could do was stare into his blazing eyes. Then, without warning, he smashed his lips onto mine, drowning me in a passionate and angry-fuelled searing hot kiss.

Chapter 9

Andriana

The cold stone wall pressed against my back, but the heat of the argument still lingered between Nathaniel and me. His body pinned mine, his hands firmly gripping my wrists above my head, his vivid green eyes locked onto my defiant blue ones. I could feel the tension radiating off him, a primal energy that set my nerves on fire.

"Dammit, Andriana," he growled, his jaw clenched in frustration. "Do you have any idea how reckless you've been?" My heart raced as I stared into his eyes, feeling the electric charge between us grow unbearable. Nathaniel's mouth crushed mine, hungry and demanding, his hands roaming my body. I threaded my fingers through his dark hair and wrapped my legs around his waist, pressing myself against his rapidly growing hardness. He grabbed my ass, grinding me into the wall. I moaned, arching into him, wanting more. His lips trailed down my neck, nipping and sucking. My head fell back as he found the spot where my neck and shoulder met, that sensitive place that drove me wild. He sucked hard, and I cried out, shuddering. The slight pain mixed with pleasure, the sensations swirling together and pooling between my legs. I rocked my hips, desperate for friction, and Nathaniel growled. His hands slid under my shirt, calloused palms skimming up my sides. He cupped my breasts, squeezing and kneading before tugging down my bra. His mouth closed over one nipple, licking and sucking, while he pinched and rolled the other between his fingers. I squirmed and panted, intoxicated by the feel of his mouth and hands on my skin. I didn't know how, but even though we had just met he knew just how to touch me, how to make me come undone for him. My hands fisted in his hair, holding him in place as he lavished attention on my breasts. Unable to resist any longer, I pulled my wrists free from his grasp and grabbed the back of his neck, pulling his mouth back up to mine. Our lips crashed together, the ferocity of our passion fuelled by the anger still simmering beneath the surface. When he finally broke the kiss, his eyes glowed gold with desire.

"You're mine," he rasped, voice rough with passion. He ground his hips into me again, emphasising his point.

"Yes," I breathed. I was his, just as he was mine. We belonged to each other, heart, body and soul. He kissed me again, hard and hungry, before carrying me off to our room to continue what we'd started. Our argument now long forgotten, replaced by the fierce passion that burned between us.

Nathaniel lifted me away from the wall and his strong arms cradled me as he carried me effortlessly across the dimly lit basement, his eyes locked onto mine with a predatory intensity that sent shivers down my spine. My heart pounded in my chest, the anticipation of what was to come heightening my senses.

"Here," he growled, reaching a large wooden table, and with one powerful sweep of his arm, he cleared its surface, sending clutter crashing to the floor. The sound echoed throughout the room, a testament to the raw passion driving us both. He laid me down on the cold tabletop, my back pressing against the smooth surface. His hands were everywhere, stroking and caressing as he kissed down the column of my throat. I arched into his touch, craving more. My shirt was torn open, buttons scattering across the table and floor. I didn't care. All that mattered was Nathaniel's hands on my bare skin and his mouth claiming mine again. Our kiss was hungry and desperate. Teeth clashed and tongues tangled as we devoured each other. He made short work of my bra, flinging the scrap of lace aside before pinching and rolling my nipples. I moaned into his mouth, pleasure shooting straight to my core. My jeans and panties were ripped away next, leaving me naked and exposed to his gaze. But there was no shame, only burning need. His gaze raked over my body, taking in every inch of me as if memorising each curve and contour. I felt the heat of his stare as surely as if his touch grazed my flesh, and it sent a thrill coursing through me. This man, this powerful Alpha, he wanted me with an intensity that matched my own desires.

"Beautiful," he murmured, his voice rough with need. The praise sent a flush of warmth across my cheeks, and I found myself arching my back, silently begging for his touch.

"Please, Nathaniel," I whispered, unable to contain the longing in my voice. "I need you."

My heart raced as Nathaniel knelt between my legs, his powerful hands gripping my thighs and spreading them apart. His eyes were dark with desire, locking onto mine for a moment before he lowered his head to place a searing kiss on my inner thigh. I shivered at the sensation, feeling the heat of his lips against my sensitive flesh.

"Look at you," he murmured, his voice thick with lust. "So wet and ready for me." His words sent an electric jolt through my body, and I bit my lip to suppress a moan. My fingers curled into the cold surface of the table, desperate for something to hold on to as Nathaniel continued his sensual assault. As Nathaniel trailed kisses up my trembling legs, I could feel my arousal building, pooling in my core like molten lava. It was almost too much to bear, and I found myself shifting restlessly beneath him, seeking relief from the delicious ache that threatened to consume me.

"Please," I begged, my voice breathless with need. "I can't take it anymore."

"Is that so?" Nathaniel asked, raising an eyebrow as he cast a smouldering look in my direction.

"What do you want me to do, love? Tell me."

"Touch me," I whispered, my cheeks flushing with embarrassment even as my body cried out for his touch. "Taste me."

"As you wish, my little witch," he replied, and without another word, he lowered his head to my throbbing centre. The moment his tongue made contact with my swollen clit, I gasped, feeling as if I'd been struck by lightning.

Nathaniel wasted no time, swirling his tongue around my sensitive nub, teasing me mercilessly as he continued to spread my slick folds with his strong fingers.

"God, you taste incredible," he groaned, his hot breath against my soaked flesh causing me to shiver with anticipation. As Nathaniel continued to lavish attention on my aching core, his tongue delving deeper into me, I could feel the pressure building within my body. My hips bucked against his face, desperate for more as he brought me closer and closer to the edge.

"Please," I cried out, my fingers tangling in his hair, urging him on. "Don't stop."

"Never," he promised, his voice muffled by my wetness. His tongue flicked and swirled, sending me spinning toward an orgasm that threatened to tear me apart.

"Fuck, Nathaniel!" I screamed, my vision blurring as the world around me shattered, leaving only pleasure in its wake. My body shook uncontrollably as I rode the waves of ecstasy that washed over me, my moans echoing throughout the basement. As my climax began to subside, I felt Nathaniel's lips press gently against my trembling flesh, soothing me as I struggled to catch my breath. My body still hummed with aftershocks, and I knew then that this was only the beginning of our passionate connection.

Nathaniel looked up at me with a wicked glint in his eyes. He began to move up my body, his lips blaze a trail of fire up my torso, teeth nipping sharply at my flesh. I arched into his touch with a gasp, hands fisting in his hair.

"Nathaniel..." His name came out as a plea, my body already aching with renewed need. Our intention to join had only sharpened my hunger for him, not sated it. I craved the feel of his skin against mine, the thrust of his body in mine; I needed him with a desperation that bordered on madness. Perhaps he sensed it, for Nathaniel growled against my breast and surged up to capture my mouth in a searing kiss. Our tongues duelled and danced as his hands roamed my body, stroking and squeezing my curves possessively. I could feel his erection pressed against my thigh, hot and heavy, and I rocked my hips to grind against it in silent entreaty.

Nathaniel broke the kiss with a snarl, eyes glowing bright.

"So impatient, little witch. Must I teach you patience?" His hand slipped between my legs to cup me intimately, middle finger sliding through my slick folds to circle my clit. I cried out at the sensation, back arching.

"Please!" The word was wrenched from me as Nathaniel began to move his finger in slow, deliberate circles. I was already sensitive from my last climax and teetering on the edge of another. My hands clawed at his shoulders, nails biting into his flesh. I yanked Nathaniel down by his hair, crushing my mouth to his. The kiss was hungry and desperate, all teeth and tongue as I tried to convey my need. Nathaniel growled into my mouth but did not deny me, kissing me back with equal ferocity. His finger moved faster between my legs and I broke the kiss to throw my head back with a wail. My inner walls clenched down on nothing, aching to be filled, and Nathaniel took advantage of my exposed throat to nip sharply at it. The twin sensations of his bite and the circling of his finger sent me tumbling over the edge with a scream. My back bowed as pleasure blew out my senses, and my inner muscles spasmed powerfully.

Through the haze of my climax I felt Nathaniel shift, and then the broad head of his cock was nudging at my entrance.

"Are you ready, little witch?" he asked through gritted teeth, his desire for me painfully evident in his voice.

"More than ready," I breathed, my own need overwhelming me. "Please, Nathaniel... I need you inside me." With a growl, Nathaniel thrust into me without warning, and I gasped at the sudden fullness, feeling both deliciously stretched and filled by him. He wasted no time, beginning to fuck me hard, each powerful thrust sending waves of pleasure coursing through my body.

"Goddess, Nathaniel..." I moaned, digging my nails into his shoulders, urging him to go even harder. My body burned with desire, every nerve ending alive and screaming for release. Nathaniel responded to my pleas, his pace becoming rougher, more demanding. As we moved together, our bodies slick with sweat, the rickety table beneath us creaked in protest. The table gave a sudden sharp crack and collapsed beneath us. We crashed to the floor, Nathaniel twisting at the last moment to avoid crushing me. Laughter bubbled up in my chest, even as Nathaniel began to move again. There was something absurd and wonderful about this moment, about the two of us ravaging each other with such abandon that we broke furniture. Nathaniel's lips curved in a smile, eyes glinting with humour and heat.

"Careful, witch. At this rate we'll destroy the entire house."

"Promises, promises," I teased, rocking my hips to meet his thrusts. The new angle sent starbursts of pleasure ricocheting through me, ratcheting the tension coiling in my stomach ever higher. Nathaniel growled again, the sound rumbling up from deep in his chest. His hips pistoned faster, fingers digging into my hips hard enough to leave bruises.

"Come for me, my perfect little witch," he commanded, his voice hoarse with lust. "Let me feel you come undone." His words were all I needed, and I surrendered to the tidal wave of ecstasy that washed over me. My orgasm roared through my body like wildfire, consuming me entirely as I clung to him.

The intensity of our connection sent shivers down my spine, and I could feel something deep within me reaching out to Nathaniel. pleasure and magic swirling through and around us in an endless feedback loop. His cock had stretched and filled me, the thick ridge rasping over sensitive tissues with every stroke.

"So perfect," he groaned, hips snapping forward. My nails had raked down his back and he snarled, fangs grazing my throat in warning and promise. The coil of tension in my stomach wound tighter and tighter, heat suffusing my body until I felt I would combust from the inside out. It was as if my very soul was yearning for him, hungering to become one with this powerful, enigmatic man.

"Goddess, Nathaniel," I gasped, barely able to form coherent words through the haze of pleasure that clouded my mind. "I need you... I need this bond... so much."

"Let it happen, witch," he urged, his breath hot against my ear as he continued to thrust into me mercilessly. "Let our souls become one."

His words sent a shockwave through me, pushing me closer and closer to the edge. My climax built like a storm inside me, growing in strength until I couldn't hold back any longer.

"Fuck, Nathaniel!" I screamed, my entire body tensing as the orgasm ripped through me, stars bursting behind my eyes. I felt my essence intertwine with Nathaniel's, creating a connection so powerful and profound it threatened to consume me entirely. Nathaniel reacted to my overwhelming passion, his own release nearing. His grip on me tightened, muscles tensing as he found his own release, spilling his seed deep within me. As our bodies trembled together, he bit down on my neck, marking me as his own. The sensation of his teeth sinking into my flesh only intensified the fusion of our essences, solidifying the mate bond between us. The mate bond flared to life, a golden thread connecting our souls. I gasped at the intimacy of it, Nathaniel's love and desire and bone-deep satisfaction echoing through me.

I laid there panting, trying to catch my breath, heart pounding as I stared up at the ceiling. The mate bond thrummed between us, a conduit of love and desire and bone-deep satisfaction. Nathaniel rolled to his side, pulling me against his chest. I went willingly, craving his touch and the warmth of his body.

"You're mine now, little witch," he had rasped, nosing at the mark on my neck. It had tingled pleasantly, a sign of the bond we now shared.

"For as long as we both shall live."

"And beyond my wolf," I replied with a smile. "And you're mine," The alpha wolf inside him preened at the claim, wolf and man both revelling in their conquest. I trailed my fingers down his cheek, marvelling at how perfectly we fit. Two halves of a whole. Puzzle pieces.

"Partners." His lips curved in a soft smile.

"Partners," he agreed. "My mate. My equal in all things." Joy swelled within me, brighter than the sun. The future was ours, and it would be glorious. Nathaniel kissed me then, slow and sweet and brimming with promise. I melted into him with a sigh, the mate bond singing between us. We had eternity to explore the depths of our connection. But for now, I was content to remain here in his arms, the rest of the world fading away.

Chapter 10

Andriana

The taste of Nathaniel's lips still lingered on mine as we dressed, pulling our clothes back on piece by piece. The rush of our union was quickly replaced with a sense of urgency as we needed to finish setting up the little room in the basement for Gayle. As we worked together, cleaning up the broken parts of the table, we couldn't help but exchange soft, loving smiles and tender caresses. It was almost as if our newfound connection amplified every touch and glance.

"Here," Nathaniel said, his voice low and warm as he handed me a broom to sweep away the shattered wood that littered the floor. "We should be able to get this place cleaned up in no time."

"Thank you," I murmured. My fingers brushed against his as I took the broom from him, sending a shiver down my spine. Even mundane tasks like cleaning seemed charged with new energy now that we were bonded.

As we finished tidying the room, Nathaniel and I moved a spare mattress into it, positioning it carefully in the corner. I could tell he shared my concern for Gayle, his strong jaw set with determination.

"We can't risk anything else happening to her, especially after she broke the window upstairs," I told him, my voice laced with worry. "Until the spell is out of her system, we can't give her anything to hurt herself with."

"Agreed," Nathaniel replied, his eyes meeting mine. There was a depth of understanding and compassion in his gaze that made me fall even more in love with him. "We'll make sure she's safe and sound." As we surveyed the finished room, I felt a swell of gratitude for Nathaniel and the bond we had formed. Together, we would face any challenge that came our way – including helping Gayle through her ordeal.

"Thank you for being here with me," I whispered, reaching up to press a gentle kiss to the corner of his mouth. "Together, we'll overcome anything that comes our way."

"Always," Nathaniel promised, his arms wrapping around me in a warm embrace. Our bond had only just begun, but already it felt like an unbreakable force.

Feeling the lingering warmth from Nathaniel's embrace, I led him upstairs to the guest room where Gayle was sleeping. As we entered the softly lit room, Becca and Trenton sat in a corner, their heads close together as they whispered quietly. Their eyes flicked towards us and knowing smiles spread across their faces. My cheeks flushed with embarrassment, realising that the sounds of our passionate love making must have reached their ears.

"Ahem," I cleared my throat nervously, trying to regain some composure. "How is she?"

"Still sleeping," Becca answered, her voice gentle. "She hasn't stirred since you left."

"Good," I sighed, relief washing over me. "We've set up a safer space for her downstairs." As I spoke, my hand instinctively rose to cover the mate bond mark on my neck, but Nathaniel caught my wrist, his grip firm yet tender.

"Don't act ashamed, little witch," he scolded me, his voice low and sensual. "Fate is the most natural process there is." I looked into his eyes, seeing the love and conviction within them.

"I'm not ashamed," I admitted, my voice barely above a whisper. "Just... maybe a little overwhelmed." Nathaniel's lips curved into a soft smile, understanding filling his gaze.

"That's normal," he assured me. "But we'll get through this together."

"Thank you," I murmured, leaning into him for a moment, drawing strength from his presence.

"Let's move Gayle to the new room," Trenton suggested, rising from his seat. He glanced at Nathaniel, silently asking for assistance.

"Of course," Nathaniel agreed, his voice steady and confident. With a nod from Nathaniel, he gently scooped Gayle into his strong arms, cradling her as if she were made of porcelain. I followed closely behind, my heart pounding in my chest like a wild drum. As we descended the stairs, the dimly lit basement loomed before us like an ominous cavern, casting eerie shadows on the stone walls.

The moment Trenton set Gayle down onto the makeshift mattress, her eyes snapped open, wide with terror. A blood-curdling scream erupted from her lips, echoing through the cold chamber.

"Gayle!" I shouted, rushing to her side, my voice cracking with desperation. "It's okay, you're safe." Becca joined me, placing a reassuring hand on Gayle's shoulder.

"We're here for you, Gayle," she added softly, her eyes filled with concern.

"Stay away from me!" Gayle shrieked, her breath coming in ragged, uneven gasps. Her gaze darted around the room frantically, finally landing on the mark adorning my neck. Her expression twisted with disgust, and my stomach clenched at the venomous words that spilled from her mouth.

"You dirty whore," she spat, glaring at me with unbridled hatred. "You let that mutt brand you with his mark, connecting yourself to him?" I recoiled, feeling as though I'd been slapped across the face. My cheeks burned with shame and hurt, and I struggled to hold back the tears that threatened to fall.

"Gayle... I-" I stammered, searching for something to say, but she wasn't finished.

"Is this what you've become?" she hissed, her eyes narrowing. "A pathetic plaything for some filthy beast?" Unable to bear the cruel words of my once dear friend, I turned and fled from the room, my vision blurred by tears I could no longer contain.

I stumbled out of the basement, my heart pounding in my chest. Behind me, I heard Becca's voice as she closed and locked the door to the little room where we'd left Gayle. The click of the lock seemed to echo through the house, hitting me like a physical blow.

"Hey, Andriana," Becca called softly, catching up to me in the hallway. She pulled me into a tight hug, her arms warm and comforting around me. "Don't listen to her, alright? You know that's not who you are." I nodded, though the hurt still gnawed at me. I knew Gayle wasn't herself right now, but her words had cut deep all the same. I couldn't shake the feeling that there was some truth in her accusations, that maybe I had been too quick to give myself over to Nathaniel.

"Come on," Nathaniel said, stepping closer and offering a hand to me. His touch sent a shiver down my spine, an almost electric sensation that both soothed and excited me. "You've had a long day; let me take you to bed." I raised an eyebrow at him, half-amused despite the turmoil within me. He chuckled, a deep, rumbling sound that vibrated through my core.

"Just to sleep," he reassured me, his golden-brown eyes holding mine with a tender gaze. "At least for now."

"Alright," I agreed, allowing him to lead me upstairs. We passed by another guest room where Becca and Trenton were settling in for the night, exchanging quiet words and soft smiles. Seeing them together brought a small measure of comfort to me, knowing that I wasn't alone in navigating the complex web of emotions that had entangled us all.

When we reached my room, Nathaniel held the door open for me, his strong hand resting gently on my lower back as I stepped inside. The familiar scent of lavender and vanilla filled my nostrils, a soothing reminder of the sanctuary this room had always been for me.

"Thank you," I whispered as Nathaniel pulled back the covers on my bed, revealing the soft, inviting sheets beneath. He helped me under the blankets before climbing in beside me. His body was warm and solid against my own, and I couldn't deny the sense of safety that washed over me simply being near him.

"Sleep now," he murmured, his breath tickling my ear as he drew me close, wrapping his arms around me. My head rested on his chest, the steady rhythm of his heartbeat a comforting lullaby that soon lulled me into a deep slumber.

My dreams were haunted by darkness, a thick fog that seemed to close in on me from all directions. Panic bubbled up within me as I stumbled through the void, my heart pounding wildly in my chest. The air felt heavy and oppressive, weighing down on me like a physical force. Inky tendrils snaked out from the shadows, reaching for me with their chilling touch.

"Help!" I cried out, but my voice was swallowed by the miasma, leaving only silence in its wake.

Just when I thought I would be consumed by the darkness, a flickering light appeared in the distance, a beacon of hope amidst the suffocating gloom. It was a fire, its flames licking hungrily at the edges of the night, illuminating the silhouette of a town engulfed in its inferno. As I approached, my relief turned to horror when I noticed a shadowy figure stalking through the burning streets. It moved with predatory grace, its every step radiating menace and power.

When it turned toward me, I froze, unable to tear my gaze away from the eyes that locked onto mine. Copper flecks swirled within their golden brown depths, drawing me in even as terror clawed desperately at my insides. The creature lunged at me, a guttural growl tearing from its throat.

My scream echoed through the night, shattering the illusion as I bolted upright in bed. Nathaniel's arms were around me in an instant, his soothing presence anchoring me to reality.

"What's wrong?" he asked, concern etched into his features.

"I-I had a nightmare," I stammered, trembling as the remnants of fear clung to me like cobwebs. "I don't think it's over, Nathaniel. Something is still out there." His eyes held mine, steady and reassuring. "We'll figure things out in the morning, love," he promised. "Try to get some sleep. I'm here, and I won't let anything hurt you."

I wanted to believe him, but the shadows lurking at the edges of my mind refused to be banished so easily. They whispered of danger and secrets yet to be uncovered, a persistent reminder that we were far from safe.

"Alright," I murmured, allowing Nathaniel to pull me back into his embrace. As I closed my eyes, I tried to focus on the warmth of his body against mine, the steady rhythm of his heartbeat beneath my ear. But as I drifted off once more, I couldn't shake the feeling that something was waiting for us in the darkness, poised to strike when we least expected it.

I tried to listen to Nathaniel's advice and let sleep claim me once more, but the ghostly echoes of Myron's prophecy swirled through my thoughts like a relentless storm. The sense of foreboding grew stronger with each passing moment, gnawing at the edges of my consciousness until I could no longer ignore it. Gently extricating myself from Nathaniel's embrace, I slid out of bed and padded softly towards the door. A brief pang of guilt tugged at my heart as I left him sleeping peacefully, but I knew that I couldn't rest until I had some answers. With a silent vow to return soon, I slipped out of the room and made my way downstairs.

The familiar scent of old parchment and ancient magic greeted me as I entered the living room, the shelves lining the walls filled to capacity with the accumulated knowledge of generations. Dim moonlight filtered in through the windows, casting eerie shadows on the floor as I began my search.

"Come on, Andriana," I muttered under my breath, pulling one dusty tome after another from their resting places. "There has to be something here." Hours slipped by unnoticed as I delved into the depths of my ancestors' wisdom, seeking any mention of the prophecy that haunted me. My eyes grew gritty and sore from straining to read the faded ink by the meagre light, but I refused to give up. If there was even the slightest chance that I could find the answers we needed, then I owed it to everyone, to Nathaniel, to our future child, and to myself, to keep searching.

As the first pale fingers of dawn began to creep across the sky, I came across an ancient volume with an ornate cover, bound in worn leather and adorned with intricate symbols. A shiver of recognition danced down my spine as I traced the embossed title with trembling fingers: The Dark Prophecies: Visions from the Essence of the Fates. A sudden certainty filled me, and my pulse quickened with anticipation.

"Please," I whispered, opening the book with reverent care. "Let this be it."

As I continued to read, I couldn't help but roll my eyes at the dramatic language and flowery prose that seemed to pervade these old texts. So many claimed to be the words of some Oracle or other - all grandiose and mysterious, but ultimately empty.

But then, a passage leaped out at me, sending shivers down my spine. It spoke of shadowed chambers, cosmic weaves, and the Grand Enigma, an ageless riddle that lay at the heart of existence itself. But one sentence stood out over all

"These fragments, the scattered shards of reality's mirror, are but the puzzle pieces of existence, each one a part of the All, yet isolated and concealed."

This was what I had been searching for, the elusive thread that connected everything.

"Goddess," I whispered, my breath catching in my throat, "this is it." With renewed determination, I began to search through the text more earnestly, trying to discern the hidden wisdom that would illuminate the path I needed to follow. The words seemed to dance before my eyes, creating a mesmerising symphony of light and shadow, chaos and order.

"Embrace the paradox," I murmured, echoing the text. "Only then shall you transcend the limitations of your transient existence and glimpse the eternal truth."

As I continued to delve deeper into the mysterious world of The Dark Prophecies, I could feel the weight of destiny pressing down upon me, urging me to unlock the hidden connections that would reveal the true nature of my fate.

"Seek them with a pure heart," I recited, my voice barely more than a whisper. "And the Dark Prophecies shall unfold their wisdom, revealing visions from the Essence of Fates." I knew then that I was on the precipice of something monumental, a revelation that could change the course of my life and the lives of those around me.

Hours had slipped by without my notice as I fervently searched for the prophecy. My fingers brushed against the ancient pages, tenderly turning them, feeling their worn edges. The dim light from the lamp flickered in the darkened living room, casting eerie shadows that seemed to dance upon the walls. The weight of the knowledge contained within these mystical tomes pressed heavily on me, but it was a burden I was determined to bear.

My heart leaped when I finally found what I had been seeking, the prophecy. The words swam before my eyes, a blend of hope and fear. As I committed the lines to memory, the sound of footsteps echoed through the hallway, breaking my concentration. Startled, I glanced up to see Nathaniel descending the stairs, his countenance etched with concern.

"Adriana, it's early," he said softly, his brow furrowed. "You should still be in bed." Tears welled in my eyes, and I met his gaze, unable to contain the overwhelming tide of emotions within me.

"Nathaniel, I found it," I whispered, my voice trembling. "The prophecy..."

The Prophecy of the Keystone

In the world where shadows blend with light,
A maiden of twenty-five shall rise from the night.
Descendant of Diana, Queen of Witches and Beasts,
Half witch, half wolf, her lineage in the least.

From an alpha's might and a priestess concealed,
Her ancient bloodline to the goddess revealed.
Though the paths of magic run deep in her veins,
Her true power's asleep, bound by invisible chains.

For the key to her strength, the heart's true desire,
Lies in a bond, set passionately on fire.
Born of two worlds, she's a hybrid so rare,
Destined to change fates, with power to bear.

She'll encounter a man, from realms dark or light,

BOUND BY PROPHECY

His submission to her, sets their spirits alight.
For in their union, the scales shall tip,
Balancing power, in a tight-knit grip.

If he's born of the light, the world finds its peace,
If of darkness, then shadows may never cease.
But remember this well, for as stories unfold,
The key to their fate, in their hands, they do hold.

Butterflies emerge, symbols of transformation,
Guiding their journey, without hesitation.
Balance is crucial, for the stakes are so high,
The gods watching closely with a vigilant eye.

So, heed this prophecy, for as legends declare,
Love and choice rule over despair, with Diana's care.

Chapter 11

Andriana

Four years later

In the last four years since my life became entwined with Nathaniel's we married and built a beautiful life together, our love crossing the boundaries of witch and werewolf. Our small Victorian home nestled within the Lake Key Coven was a testament to our union, where I served as their Priestess. We divided our time between his pack and my coven, creating a mingled existence that was frowned upon by the general witch community. But we were happy, and that was all that mattered.

My days, though, were consumed by the Dark Prophecies book and the prophecy about my future child. I poured over every word, every cryptic verse, searching for answers and meaning. Nathaniel was ever-supportive, reassuring me that together, we would figure it out. I thought that we would have more time but recent news had brought the matter crashing to the forefront of both of our minds.

Which was the reason why Gayle sat stiffly on the sofa in front of me, her eyes narrowed and her mouth set in a hard line. Beside her, little Audrey,

Gayle's three-year-old daughter, perched on the edge of her seat, her bright blue eyes fixed on the plate of biscuits on the coffee table. The child's raven black hair framed her face in soft curls, only accentuating her mischievous expression.

As I watched from my armchair, it broke my heart to see Gayle acting with such coldness towards her own daughter. It was as if she couldn't bear to look at the girl, a painful reminder of the trauma she had endured at Myron's hands. But I couldn't help but smile at Audrey's plucky spirit; she seemed undeterred by her mother's frosty demeanour.

After it had taken myself, Becca and others from my coven almost a month to drain the compulsion spell from Gayle's system, Gayle had left my house, telling me she never wanted to see me again. It was her mother that had phoned me two months later to tell me that Gayle was now pregnant and wouldn't tell her mother who the father was. I explained what happened and if I expected any sort of sympathy for the ordeal her daughter went through, then I would have been very disappointed. Miriam simply said that it was no wonder that Gayle wouldn't tell her what had happened, she would have been ashamed to be caught in a sorcerer spell as well. It was only through other witches that I heard that Gayle was made to prove her worth to her mother before her mother would allow her to take the title of the High Priestess.

"Gayle," I began, hoping to smooth things over, "I understand that this is difficult for you, but we need your support. This union between our coven and the pack will bring us greater strength."

"Strength?" Gayle scoffed, her eyes flashing with anger. "You really believe that fraternising with mutts will make you stronger? If anything, it will weaken you, dilute your power powers and taint our bloodlines."

"Times are changing, Gayle," I implored. "We can't afford to cling to old prejudices. We need each other, witches, werewolves, all magical beings, if we're going to survive in this world."

Before Gayle could retort, Audrey made a bold move. With surprising speed, she darted her hand towards the plate of biscuits, eager to claim another treat. She almost succeeded, but Gayle's hand shot out like lightning, slapping her daughter's wrist.

"Sit still, you little brat!" she hissed, her face contorted with anger. Audrey blinked back tears, but then defiantly stuck out her tongue at her mother. She quickly snatched a biscuit and bolted from the room, laughter echoing behind her.

"Let her be, Gayle," I said gently, placing a calming hand on her arm as she made to follow Audrey. "She'll be perfectly safe out there."

"Safe?" Gayle huffed, her eyes narrowing in disdain. "With all these... mutts around? It would serve her right if she got eaten by one of them." I bit my lip, trying to suppress my anger at her words. Even after everything that had happened, Gayle still refused to see the good in the Half Moon pack, the werewolves who had stood by us and helped save her from Myron's clutches.

"Gayle, you know that's not true," I replied softly, choosing my words carefully. "The pack has been nothing but kind and supportive towards us. They're not the monsters you think they are." I tried to inject a note of calm into my voice. "But you must remember that if it wasn't for those 'mutts,' as you call them, we wouldn't have been able to save you from Myron." Her blue eyes flashed with anger, and she glared at me.

"If it wasn't for you getting me involved with that other pack in the first place, neither of us would have been on Myron's radar at all!" I clenched my fists, struggling to maintain my composure. I wanted to remind her that she had invited herself into the mix, but I knew it would fall on deaf ears.

Instead, I took a deep breath and searched for another way to reach her.

"Gayle, everything I've done has been to protect our people and to strengthen the bonds between us. We can't afford to be divided, not now, not when the world is changing so rapidly around us."

"By joining forces with werewolves?" she scoffed, shaking her head. "You're deluded, Andriana. The goddess never intended for us to mingle with such creatures. They're animals, Andriana, nothing more than savage beasts who would turn on us in a heartbeat if it suited their needs."

"Is that really what you think?" I asked, my heart aching at her stubbornness. "Or are you just unable to see past your own prejudices?"

"Watch your tongue, Andriana," she warned, her voice cold and sharp. "I am still the High Priestess of the UK witches, and I will not tolerate such insolence."

I took a deep breath knowing that what I was going to say next wouldn't go over well. I just hoped that Gayle had some sort of empathy left in her. But she never listened before, I doubt that she would now.

"Gayle, there's another reason why we need to unite the coven and the pack," I said.

"Ah, yes, the prophecy," Gayle sighed, rolling her eyes. "You're not still clinging to that nonsense, are you? Only a fool would believe anything that monster said."

"The prophecy is real!" I insisted, my voice trembling with emotion. The musty scent of ancient parchment filled my mind, a testament to the countless hours I'd spent poring over the cryptic verses within the Dark Prophecies book.

"Really?" she scoffed, her laughter harsh and mocking. "Andriana, if you truly believe that drivel pertains to you, then you have a serious case of delusion. To think that you, of all people, could be the descendant of the Essence of Diana is laughable at best."

"Please." I implored, my hands shaking as I grasped at the hope that she might understand. "You know better than anyone how powerful my bloodline is. What if it's true? What if my child is destined to change everything?"

"Oh please," Gayle said, "And how can you be so sure that your child won't bring us even more misery and destruction?"

"Because she is mine, and I have to believe that."

"Andriana you acting like there actually is a child," Gayle scoffed. I took a deep breath, knowing that this was not going the way I wanted it.

"I'm pregnant," I whispered, gathering my courage, "Charlene has seen that she is the one from the prophecy." Her eyes widened in a momentary surprise before her expression hardened again.

"Well, you shouldn't have opened your legs for the dog then, should you?" she spat venomously. My heart clenched at her cruel words, but before I could respond, a low growl echoed through the room.

Nathaniel appeared in the doorway, Audrey perched happily on his broad shoulders. Her bright blue eyes sparkled with delight as she clapped her hands together.

"Look, Mummy!" she called out to Gayle, her voice bursting with glee. "The big wolfman even growls!"

I couldn't help but smile at the innocence of the child, even as my heart ached at the rift between us all.

"Put my child down right now!" Gayle's voice trembled with anger, her face flushed a deep shade of red. Nathaniel's eyes narrowed as he gently lowered Audrey to the floor. The little girl didn't seem to notice the tension in the room, instead giggling and running circles around Nathaniel's legs.

"Your daughter is safe with me," Nathaniel said quietly, though his voice was edged with steel. He turned his glare on Gayle, asserting his dominance as Alpha even within the confines of our Victorian home. "You are a guest here, and you will not insult my mate." My chest tightened at his words, both grateful for his protection and saddened by the rift that seemed to grow wider with each passing moment. I glanced at Audrey, who continued to laugh and play, blissfully unaware of the animosity swirling around her. How could any mother say such cruel things about their own child? I couldn't help but wonder what kind of life awaited the innocent girl under Gayle's care. Gayle's eyes flashed with defiance as she met Nathaniel's gaze.

"I'll remedy that," she hissed. "I'll leave."

"Gayle, please-" I tried to interject, desperate to salvage what was left of our friendship. But she ignored me, her attention focused solely on Nathaniel.

"Stay away from my daughter," she warned him, her voice thick with contempt.

"Gayle, wait!" I called out, desperation in my voice. "Please, reconsider the witches' position on joining our coven with the pack. We need your help and support." Gayle stopped in her tracks, but refused to look at me. Her body was rigid, her disdain clear in every line of her posture.

"You expect me to condone this... abomination?" she spat, her tone dripping with venom. At that moment, I knew I had to stand firm. I could not let Gayle's prejudice destroy everything Nathaniel and I had built. So, I squared my shoulders and met her cold gaze.

"Yes," I replied, my voice steady. "I do. Because it's the right thing to do, for us and for the magical community at large." Gayle scoffed, her eyes narrowing.

"Andriana, if you go through with this, the coven will no longer be recognised by the witches. You'll all be declared rogues. Is that what you want?" Her words stung like a slap to the face, but I refused to back down. I glanced at Nathaniel, drawing strength from his unwavering support.

"If that's the price we must pay for the safety of my child, then so be it."

"Fine," she snapped, her expression cold and unforgiving. She turned and grabbed Audrey by the hand, yanking the child away from Nathaniel's side.

"Come, Audrey," she commanded, her grip tight on the girl's small hand.

"Mummy, no!" Audrey protested, struggling against her mother's grasp.

"Gayle, please don't-" I began, my heart breaking for the innocent child caught in the crossfire of our conflict.

"Goodbye, Andriana," Gayle cut me off, her voice devoid of warmth or affection. It was as if the bond we once shared had been severed completely, leaving only bitterness and resentment in its place. With that, she pulled Audrey out of the door and into the cold evening air. I watched them go, my heart aching with loss and regret. But despite the pain, I knew I couldn't let Gayle's threats deter me from the path I had chosen.

Tears streamed down my cheeks as I clung to Nathaniel, his strong arms wrapping around me like a protective shield.

"What are we going to do?" I choked out, the weight of Gayle's words settling heavily on my heart.

"Love," Nathaniel murmured into my hair, "we'll find a way through this. We have each other, and our combined strength will be enough." His words offered some comfort, but the uncertainty still gnawed at me. How could we protect our unborn child from the dark prophecy without the witches' support? Our daughter would need both her coven and pack to navigate the treacherous path that lay ahead.

A gentle knock on the door interrupted my thoughts. Wiping away my tears, I turned to see Charlene standing there, her expression apologetic.

"I'm sorry to interrupt," she said softly, avoiding my gaze. "But the meeting is about to start. We need you both at the moot hall."

"Thank you, Charlene," I replied, forcing a smile as I disentangled myself from Nathaniel's embrace.

"Let's go," Nathaniel said, taking my hand in his. Together, we stepped outside and began to make our way towards the moot hall, the crisp autumn air stinging my tear-streaked face.

Chapter 12

Andriana

As Nathaniel, Charlene, and I entered the moot main hall, I was struck by the sheer number of people gathered there. Almost 250 souls stood before us, their eyes expectant and curious. The room hummed with a nervous energy as the Half Moon pack and Lake Key coven mingled amongst one another. Werewolves numbered over the witches, their powerful forms imposing, while the witches' magical presence made them no less formidable.

"Look at how many people care about our future," Charlene whispered to me, her voice steady yet tinged with awe. I glanced at the front row where Trenton and Becca sat, their young son Christian nestled between them. His dark eyes were wide with curiosity, a brave little boy who would one day grow into a strong werewolf like his father. Further along, Marshall and his mate Amy were locked in conversation with the nine other witches from the Lake Key coven council. Their hushed voices carried an air of importance, and I couldn't help but feel the weight of their expectations on my shoulders.

"Are you ready for this?" Nathaniel's deep voice broke through my thoughts. I turned to him, searching for strength in his familiar features.

"As ready as I can be," I admitted, my voice shaky.

Charlene's serene expression flickered with determination as she gracefully made her way to one of the empty seats at the front, her long, flowing skirt trailing behind her like a cloud. Marshall, his strong jaw set firmly, stood up and called the meeting to order, his voice booming through the hall.

"Order, please! Let us begin." The chatter in the room stopped abruptly, as if someone had flipped a switch. Every pair of eyes turned to watch Nathaniel and me make our way to the front of the room. I felt my heart race, each beat reverberating in my chest, reminding me of the monumental decisions that lay ahead.

"Thank you, Marshall," Nathaniel said, his deep voice steady and commanding. "As you all know, we've gathered here today to discuss the future of our two groups, the Lake Key coven and the Half Moon pack." I glanced around the room, taking in the faces of those who meant so much to me. Trenton offered me a reassuring smile, while Becca held Christian close, her eyes filled with a mother's love and protective fierceness. The nine other witches from the council sat nearby, their expressions a mix of concern, determination, and hope.

"Your input is vital," I continued, my voice trembling slightly. "Together, we must decide how best to protect our families, our traditions, and our very existence."

"Absolutely," Nathaniel agreed, his warm hand resting on the small of my back, grounding me in the moment. "Andriana and I have some ideas that we'd like to share, but we want to hear your thoughts as well."

"Go on," Charlene encouraged, her eyes bright with curiosity. "Tell us what you're thinking."

With a deep breath, I forced my nerves to settle as Nathaniel and I stood before the room. The weight of our responsibility was palpable, but we had to be strong for our people. As the meeting began, we addressed the concerns of both the witches and werewolves in attendance. Their faces were a mix of hope and apprehension, but they listened intently to each word.

"Firstly," I said, looking around the room, "we must ensure that our territories are secure. This means strengthening our wards and increasing patrols." Nods of agreement rippled through the crowd. Werewolves shared glances with witches, the world's long-standing rivalry forgotten in this space.

"Secondly," Nathaniel continued, his voice steady and commanding, "Our strength lies in our unity, so we must work together in all aspects of our lives, not just when faced with danger." As members of both groups shared their insights and suggestions, I could see the beginnings of understanding and cooperation forming between them. There were still occasional flashes of mistrust and uncertainty, but progress was being made.

"Lastly," I said, my voice soft but firm, "we need to prepare ourselves for any challenges that may arise because of this union. We cannot afford to become complacent or underestimate our enemies."

"Indeed," Nathaniel agreed, his gaze sweeping over the room. "This is not a decision we have made lightly, but one born out of necessity. We stand at a crossroads, and the choices we make today will determine the future of our people."

For an hour, we listened to the thoughts and concerns of our community, answering questions and offering reassurance where needed. Slowly but surely, the tension in the room eased as our people came to understand and accept the necessity of our alliance. Finally, as the last of the questions were answered, I could see that our people were beginning to trust in our decision. It was a small victory, but one that filled me with hope for what lay ahead. My heart thudded in my chest, a mixture of anxiety and determination surging through me. Nathaniel's warm, reassuring gaze met mine, and he gave a subtle nod, urging me to continue. Taking a deep breath, I stood up straighter, my voice resonating throughout the hall.

"Before we end this meeting, there is one more matter we must address," I said, my blue eyes scanning the sea of faces before me. "As some of you may know, we recently received a visit from Gayle Willowvane, the High Priestess of the UK witches."

Murmurs rippled through the crowd, curiosity and concern mingling in the air as they digested this new information. I could feel the weight of their attention, heavy and expectant.

"Gayle expressed her concerns regarding our plans to merge the Lake Key coven and the Half Moon pack," I continued, my fingers twisting in my skirt as I fought to keep my composure. "She informed us that if we proceed, they will declare the witches among us rogue and receive no support from the UK witches." The room erupted in worried whispers and hushed conversations, the atmosphere thick with unease. I felt a pang of guilt for bringing such troubling news upon them, but I knew it was necessary.

"However," I said, raising my voice to command their attention once more, "Nathaniel and I have made a decision." My gaze briefly flickered towards my mate, his unwavering support giving me the strength to carry on. "Due to the circumstances surrounding my pregnancy," I hesitated a moment, feeling the life growing inside me, so small yet already so cherished, "and the prophecy that speaks of our unborn child, we believe it is our responsibility to go ahead with the merge, regardless of the consequences." I could see the fear etched across the faces of our people, but also a spark of determination, an unspoken willingness to face whatever trials lay ahead. The silence in the room was palpable, heavy with anticipation as they waited for my next words.

I took a deep breath, feeling the weight of my words as I addressed the witches in the group.

"I know that this puts you all in a terrible position," I said softly, my voice wavering with emotion. "I understand if any of you wish to move to another coven, and I will bear no ill will towards you." Nathaniel stepped forward then, his strong presence a comfort beside me.

"The same goes for any werewolf who isn't in agreement," he added, his voice firm yet gentle. "You can look to move, and I will support it. We know this will be a dangerous time for us all, and we won't judge anyone for wanting to leave." We exchanged a glance, and I nodded as he continued.

"However, for those who choose to stay, our new pack name will be the Moon Key Pack."

The room was thick with tension; the air charged with a nervous energy as countless eyes stared back at us. I could feel my heart pounding in my chest, each beat echoing through my ears like a drum. It was almost deafening.

"Is there anyone who would like to speak up?" Nathaniel asked, scanning the sea of faces before us. The silence in the room seemed to stretch on for an eternity, each second feeling like a weight pressing down on my chest. I could feel the nerves buzzing through me, my fingers twitching at my sides as I waited for someone, anyone, to break the oppressive quiet. Finally, Marshall stood up, his broad shoulders squared and confident. His warm smile was infectious, chasing away some of the tension that had been building within me.

"This pack is my family," he declared, his voice strong and resonant. "Family is the most important thing to me."

"Me too" I whispered in agreement under my breath, glancing at Nathaniel who shared a knowing nod with me. Marshall continued, gazing around the room at the faces of his friends and loved ones.

"I look forward to welcoming our Keystone Child into the world." With a determined expression, he placed his hand over his heart and recited a vow that sent shivers down my spine.

"I vow to be the sword and the shield for our Keystone Child, to fight and to stand for the Moon Key pack, no matter the cost, even unto my last dying breath." As his words echoed through the hall, the air seemed to crackle with renewed energy. His mate Amy rose to her feet, her eyes shining with conviction.

"I vow to be the sword and the shield for our Keystone Child, to fight and to stand for the Moon Key pack, no matter the cost, even unto my last dying breath," she said, her voice clear and unwavering.

My heart swelled with gratitude and pride, a lump forming in my throat as I watched our people rally together. Becca was next, her fierce loyalty shining through as she vowed to stand by me, just as I had stood by her when she needed it most. She playfully smacked Trenton on the back of his head, eliciting a chuckle from him and the crowd.

"Alright, alright," he grumbled good-naturedly, rubbing the spot where Becca had hit him. He stood, his gaze meeting mine as he spoke with sincerity.

"Not that I have any choice, but even if I did, I would still do it. I vow to be the sword and the shield for our Keystone Child, to fight and to stand for the Moon Key pack, no matter the cost, even unto my last dying breath." The energy in the room shifted as each person pledged their loyalty, making me feel surrounded by love and support. I held Nathaniel's hand tightly, my heart swelling with gratitude for these people who were willing to risk everything for our unborn child.

"Thank you," I whispered again, tears pricking at the corners of my eyes as the last few voices echoed through the room. The weight of the responsibility we all carried was daunting, yet I couldn't help but feel hopeful knowing we were united.

As the final echoes of the vows faded, I felt a small tug on my shirt. I looked down to see Christian, Becca and Trenton's son, gazing up at me with an earnest expression on his face. His eyes shone with determination, belying his young age.

"Hi, Christian," I greeted him softly, kneeling down to be at eye level with him.

"Miss Andriana," he began, his voice steady and serious. "I will grow up to be the Gamma of the pack." I could see the conviction in his gaze, as if he had seen it already etched in stone.

"Really?" I asked, touched by his sincerity.

"Uh-huh," he nodded confidently, then took a deep breath before reciting the vow like the others. "I vow to protect our Keystone Child and stand for the Moon Key pack, no matter the cost, even unto my last dying breath."

My heart felt full to bursting as I pulled him into a warm embrace, grateful for the love and support emanating not just from this little boy, but from everyone in the room. "Thank you, Christian," I whispered into his ear. He hugged me back tightly before pulling away and placing a tender kiss on my stomach.

"I already love the baby," he announced proudly, his voice filled with affection, before scampering off the stage to rejoin his parents, who were beaming with pride. As I stood up, Nathaniel placed a comforting hand on the small of my back.

"I'm so proud of them," he murmured, his voice thick with emotion as we both surveyed the room full of people who had pledged their loyalty to us and our child.

"Me too," I agreed, wiping away a stray tear that had escaped from the corner of my eye. In that moment, I knew that whatever challenges lay ahead, we would face them together, as one united Moon Key pack.

It was a few hours later, and the meeting had ended. There were only a few of us left and the atmosphere in the main hall had shifted from the earlier emotional outpouring to one of tense determination. The weight of the decisions to be made pressed down on me, a constant reminder of my responsibility to my pack and coven. Marshall, looking thoughtful, broke the uneasy silence.

"The way I see it is that if we close our territory off, no visitors at all, then we can protect our borders better." Nathaniel rubbed his temple, obviously feeling the strain of the situation. "We don't have the manpower to protect our borders and earn the money for a functioning pack. The business is still new." Amy perked up, her eyes hopeful. "What if we moved? Then they wouldn't know where to look."

"Where would we find new territory for almost 250 pack members?" Trenton countered. Amy's face fell, and I could see the disappointment etched in her features. Trenton leaned over and gave her a reassuring hug.

"But it was a good idea, little sister." Maggie chimed in with a shrug.

"It wouldn't make any difference. We are the only werewolf and witch mixed pack in existence. No matter where we are, we are going to stand out." I sighed in frustration, the enormity of our situation pressing down on me like a heavy weight. Charlene, ever the voice of reason, offered her thoughts.

"So we need to move and blend in." Nathaniel seemed to consider this.

"We can do the move. It's a stretch and would take a couple of weeks, but there is a spot that's half in the mountains that would offer us some protection." Turning and smiling at me, he added, "It even has a big lake. I bet it would shine beautifully in the moonlight." Becca's face lit up with excitement.

"I know the one! Andriana, it's the one that we played in as kids, with the stone circle hidden in it." I smiled back at them, warmth spreading through me at the thought of returning to such a cherished place from our childhood.

"Sounds perfect," I agreed. But Trenton raised another concern.

"But we are still short on men to protect our borders."

"Then we need to disappear." I looked at Charlene and the other witches, who nodded their agreement. We had previously had a discussion, one that was painful but looking more necessary.

Nathaniel furrowed his brow.

"What is it, little witch?" I turned to him, my voice steady despite the tight knot of anxiety in my chest.

"The prophecy calls for the child being born of a priestess witch and an alpha wolf, right?" Nathaniel nodded, his eyes searching mine for answers.

"What if our daughter's parents were neither of those things?" The werewolves exchanged confused glances, clearly struggling to understand where I was going with this. Trenton scratched his head, trying to make sense of it all.

"Ah, I can't claim to know much about witches, only what our Becca has told me, but I thought a priestess has a specific energy whatchamacallit?" I couldn't help but laugh at his clumsy attempt to grasp the concept.

"Yes, signature."

Charlene stepped forward, holding an ancient-looking book in her hands.

"You can hide a signature so the witch or sorcerer would only see if they searched the person themselves. If Andriana was no longer a witch, then there would be no reason to look at her."

"Andriana, you can't give up your powers!" Nathaniel exclaimed, genuine concern etched across his face. I scowled at him, determined to do whatever it took to protect my family.

"I can and I would. But what we are proposing is that if I gave off the signature of a werewolf, then there would be no reason to search me." Maggie added her thoughts.

"And, if you and Andriana were no longer the Alpha and Luna, then you wouldn't fit the prophecy."

"For that, we would do a signature switch spell," Charlene explained. She passed Nathaniel the book, who read through the passage with furrowed brows.

"It says you need two vessels and an anchor. I am one of the vessels I can see, but..." Nathaniel paused, looking unsure.

"Trenton?" I asked tentatively.

"Yes, Luna?" He replied, his expression serious.

"Will you be our Alpha?" I asked, my voice barely above a whisper.

"Of course, Luna," he responded without hesitation. Marshall interjected,

"That won't work. We would still have a witch as Luna. Maybe I would be a better choice."

"We need you as the Anchor," Charlene clarified.

"We would need to bind the witches. There are packs that have humans, so if the witches are human, then we wouldn't stand out," I suggested, trying to piece together a plan that would keep us all safe. Nathaniel summed up our discussion.

"So we are moving our territory, Trenton and I are switching positions, my mate will be a werewolf, and all of our witches will have their powers bound? Well, I guess with our new name we will be unrecognisable to outsiders." Amy asked the question on everyone's mind.

"When does it happen?"

"The majority we can do straight away, but we have to wait before we bind our powers," Becca replied, her voice steady despite the gravity of the situation.

"Until when?" Trenton inquired, looking to me for an answer. I smiled sadly, touching my stomach and meeting Nathaniel's gaze.

"Until the final witch is born."

Chapter 13

Andriana

Five Years Later

Five years had passed like the blink of an eye, and life felt more vibrant than ever. Becca had recently given birth to twins, bringing joy and excitement that echoed through our pack. The Moon Key pack was thriving in our new territory, a picturesque village surrounded by cliffs and woods, with a serene lake as its centrepiece. It seemed like only yesterday that Erica, my beautiful four-year-old daughter with Nathaniel, had filled our hearts with warmth as our newest member.

The village provided ample housing for all pack members, ensuring everyone felt secure and at ease. As we kept to ourselves, the seclusion enhanced our safety and allowed us to coexist peacefully with the outside world. To support our pack financially, Trenton, now recognised as the official Alpha, Marshal, and Nathaniel had established a successful consulting business.

"Isn't it wonderful, Andriana?" Becca's voice pulled me out of my reverie as I stood by the window, admiring the view of the village. "I can't believe how much our lives have changed since we moved here." I smiled warmly at her, my heart swelling with happiness.

"It truly is, Becca. We've come so far, and our pack has grown stronger together."

"Hey, wanna see the babies? They're finally asleep," Becca suggested, a sparkle of pride in her eyes.

"Of course," I replied, following her into the cosy nursery where the twins lay nestled in their crib.

As we stood there, watching the infants sleep peacefully, I couldn't help but reminisce about the first time I held Erica in my arms. Her bright green eyes and light red hair, so much like my own, had captivated me instantly. The love I felt for her had only grown stronger over the years.

"Your turn will come soon enough," Becca whispered, as if reading my thoughts. "Erica has been such a blessing for our pack. I can't wait to see all the amazing things she'll accomplish."

"Thank you, Becca," I replied, feeling a lump form in my throat. "I know she's destined for greatness."

"Speaking of Erica," Becca continued, grinning mischievously, "she's been so eager to meet her new playmates. I bet she's already plotting ways to wake them up." Laughter bubbled up inside me as I pictured my headstrong, spirited daughter attempting to rouse the sleeping twins. "Knowing her, she's probably got it all planned out already."

Returning to the living room, we found Trenton and Nathaniel deep in conversation about their consulting business. Their dedication to providing for the pack was truly admirable, and I couldn't be prouder.

"Everything okay?" I asked, joining them.

"Of course my love," Nathaniel replied, wrapping his arm around me. "Just discussing some ideas to expand our services."

"Sounds promising," I said encouragingly, resting my head on his shoulder. Erica came running into the room, a biscuit in her hand. She bounced into my lap and looked around.

"Where are the babies," she demanded.

"Erica, sweetie, we have to wait until the babies are awake," I told my four-year-old daughter, who was bouncing with excitement. Her light red hair danced wildly as she tried to wriggle out of my grasp and race up the stairs to the nursery.

"Mummy, please! I want to meet them now!" she pleaded, her green eyes wide and imploring. Despite her impatience, I couldn't help but smile at her enthusiasm.

"Patience, little one," I said gently, ruffling her hair and letting her squirm out of my arms again, "They'll be up soon enough."

Just then, Christian, Becca's twelve-year-old son, playfully snuck up behind Erica and tickled her sides. She squealed in delight and spun around to face him, her laughter ringing through the room like a bright melody.

"Christian, you got me!" she exclaimed, grinning from ear to ear.

"Of course I did," he replied, a mischievous glint in his eyes. "You're too easy!" Becca and I exchanged smiles as we watched the two children play. It warmed my heart to see how close they had become; Christian was fiercely protective of my little girl, and she adored him in return. Trenton had even joked that perhaps they were fated mates, destined to be together when they grew up.

"Mummy, do you think the babies will like me?" Erica asked suddenly, her voice small and uncertain.

"Of course they will, sweetheart," I reassured her, squeezing her hand gently. "You're going to be the best big cousin they could ever ask for." As she smiled up at me, hope and happiness shining in her eyes, I knew that no matter what challenges lay ahead, our bond would remain unbreakable.

While Becca and I continued chatting about the challenges of motherhood, I couldn't help but notice Erica's restlessness. Her tiny fingers fidgeted in her lap, and she kept stealing glances towards the staircase, a telltale sign of her impatience.

"Mummy, can I go see the babies now?" she asked for what seemed like the tenth time.

"Sweetie, we need to give them some more time to sleep," I replied gently, trying to keep her calm. Before I knew it, she had taken advantage of a moment when my attention was elsewhere, and her little feet pattered up the stairs. Becca and I exchanged amused glances before we heard her voice on the baby monitor, gently coaxing the twins to wake up.

"Erica!" I laughed, shaking my head as I darted up the stairs after her. "You little rascal!" I found her in the nursery, standing on her tiptoes and peering through the cot bars at Imogen and Beck. To my surprise, both babies were awake, their wide eyes watching as Erica waved her hands around excitedly.

"See, Mummy? They're awake now!" she beamed triumphantly, her cheeks flushed with excitement.

"Alright, you got me," I said, chuckling despite myself. "But just a quick visit, okay? They still need lots of rest."

"Okay, Mummy." She nodded, her eyes never leaving the twins. "Hi, Imogen! Hi, Beck! I'm your cousin Erica!" As I watched my daughter interact with the newest members of our pack, my heart swelled with love and pride.

"Mummy, guess what?" Erica suddenly exclaimed, her eyes sparkling with wonder. "The babies are magic!"

"Magic?" I asked, raising an eyebrow in curiosity. "What do you mean, sweetheart?"

"Look," she said, pointing at the twins. "I can see magic glitter on them! Imogen's is green and Beck's is blue!" I squinted my eyes, trying to see what she saw. But all I could make out were the soft, tender features of the newborns. Perhaps it was just a child's imagination at work, or maybe Erica truly had some insight into their magical potential. Either way, I felt a pang of concern for what that might mean for our pack.

"Okay, love," I said gently, placing a hand on her shoulder. "We need to leave the babies alone now. They need their rest."

"But, Mummy!" Erica protested, her bottom lip jutting out in a pout. "I just want to play with them a little more!"

"Erica, you'll have plenty of time to play with them when they're older," I insisted, my voice firm but loving. "For now, we need to let them sleep."

"Fine," she huffed, giving in. She reluctantly took my hand as I led her out of the room, casting one last longing glance back at the nursery.

As we stepped into the hallway, I couldn't shake the feeling that something was different. My daughter's words echoed in my mind, stirring up a mix of emotions within me, excitement, fear, and most of all, determination. Our family had fought hard to build this sanctuary, this haven where we could live and love freely. And if there was even the slightest chance that our newest members held some kind of power within them, I knew we would do whatever it took to protect them, and each other.

"Come on, Erica," I said, squeezing her hand gently. "Let's go find something fun to do together."

"Okay, Mummy," she agreed, her eyes lighting up once more as we made our way back downstairs.

Descending the stairs, I glanced over at Christian, who was lounging on the couch, his eyes flicking between a book and the playful antics of Erica. The bond that had formed between them was heartwarming, and I couldn't help but smile as I approached.

"Christian," I called gently, drawing his attention away from his reading. "Would you mind taking Erica to the lake to play for a bit?"

"Of course not," he replied, grinning at me before turning to Erica. "Hey, wanna race to the lake?"

"Sure!" she exclaimed, her earlier dismay forgotten as excitement lit up her face. "But I'm gonna win!"

"Ha! We'll see about that," Christian challenged, and with a shared laugh, they dashed out of the room together. I watched them go, my heart swelling with love and affection for these two young souls who brought so much joy to our lives. When the sound of their laughter faded, the room felt suddenly quiet, the weight of Erica's revelation settling heavily upon me.

"Did I hear right on the monitor?" Becca asked, concern etched into her features as she stood beside me. "Erica said the babies have magic?" I nodded, my gaze fixed on the now empty doorway.

"She said she saw glitter on them, green for Imogen, blue for Beck," I murmured, replaying the scene in my mind. "It makes sense, though. The twins didn't exist when we bound everyone's magic, so theirs wouldn't be bound either." Becca's brow furrowed, worry knitting itself into her expression.

"What are we going to do? If their magic is unbound..."

"I'll arrange a circle with the council," I assured her, determination hardening my own features. "We'll figure out how to bind their magic along with everyone else's. We've come too far to let anything jeopardise the safety and peace we've built."

"Thank you," Becca whispered, her eyes glistening with unshed tears. "Andriana, I... I just want my babies to be safe. We all do."

The evening air was thick with tension as the twelve witches gathered in my study, their faces sombre and determined. I could almost feel the magic simmering beneath the surface, a force that we had been forced to suppress for far too long.

"Binding the twins' powers won't be easy," one of the witches, Selene, spoke up, her dark eyes filled with concern. "We can't do it unless we unbind ourselves first." A murmur of agreement rippled through the room, and I nodded gravely. We all knew the risks involved in undoing our own bindings, but there was no other way. The safety of Becca's children, and indeed, our entire community, depended on it. All twelve of us must be involved to unbind ourselves, or Erica would have to activate her Hybrid powers. But since Erica wouldn't be doing that anytime soon it fell on us twelve to get done. Once we've done that, we can bind the power of everyone in the pack, including the babies.

"Then that's what we'll do," I declared, my voice steady despite the knot of anxiety tightening in my chest. "

"Time is of the essence," another witch, Carol, reminded us. "We need to act quickly in case Myron has anyone in the area looking for witches."

"An hour, maximum," I estimated, trying to instill confidence in my fellow witches. "That should be enough time for us to unbind our powers, bind the twins', and then rebind ourselves."

"Let's get started," Selene urged, rising from her seat and taking her place in the circle we formed around the room. One by one, the other witches followed suit, their expressions resolute as they prepared themselves for the task ahead.

"Focus," I instructed, taking a deep breath to calm my racing heart. "We need to be in perfect harmony for this to work."

As the circle closed, I could feel the energy building between us, a palpable force that seemed to crackle in the air. It was like a long-forgotten friend, a connection that had been severed but now yearned to be reunited.

"Remember," I whispered, my gaze locked on each of my fellow witches in turn. "We do this for the safety of our pack and the future of our children. We cannot fail."

The twelve of us stood in a circle, hands joined, as the flickering candlelight cast eerie shadows on our faces. The tension in the room was palpable, but I could sense the unyielding determination in each witch's eyes.

"Ready?" I asked, my voice steady despite the thundering of my heart. A chorus of affirmations answered me, and we began the intricate process of unravelling the binding spell that held our powers captive. As I chanted the ancient words, I felt it, the surge of magic coursing through me like a tidal wave, setting my nerves alight with a sensation I'd almost forgotten. It was exhilarating, terrifying, and a poignant reminder of what we had sacrificed for the safety of our pack. As much as I yearned to bask in the freedom of unbridled magic, I knew that we couldn't afford to indulge ourselves.

"Quickly," I urged, my voice tinged with urgency. "We must bind everyone again before it's too late." The witches moved with practised efficiency, drawing upon the power they had just reclaimed to forge new chains around the magic of every witch in the pack. Beads of sweat dotted foreheads as strain crept into their expressions, but there was no wavering, only a fierce resolve to protect those who depended on us.

"Almost there," I whispered, my pulse racing as we neared the completion of the spell. But something felt wrong; a prickling sensation crawled up my spine, warning me that all was not well.

And then Charlene cried out, her anguished scream slicing through the air like a knife. I rushed to her side, fear clawing at my chest, but she waved me off with a trembling hand.

"Finish the spell!" she gasped, her face twisted with pain and terror. My heart clenched, but I knew she was right, we couldn't afford to let our efforts come to naught.

"Keep going!" I shouted, and the other witches redoubled their efforts, the air thick with power as they wove the final strands of the binding spell. When it was done, we turned our attention to Charlene, who lay gasping on the floor. Her eyes were wide with fear as she looked up at us, her words like a chilling wind that sapped the warmth from my bones.

"I don't think we were in time."

Chapter 14

Andriana

Just under a year had passed since Charlene's frightful vision, and the Moon Key pack was on edge. The once carefree laughter that filled our home now carried a tinge of unease, and the only comfort we found was in the arms of those we held dear.

"Mummy, why is everyone so scared?" Erica asked me one evening as I tucked her into bed, her green eyes searching mine for answers.

"Sweetheart, we're just being cautious, that's all," I replied, smoothing her light red hair before placing a gentle kiss on her forehead. "Now get some sleep, okay?"

"Okay, Mummy," she whispered, snuggling deeper into her blankets. But I knew my little girl was very much aware of the tension that encased our pack.

I still remembered the night Charlene had shared her vision with us, an attack on our pack with many lives lost. She had cried for hours afterward, and it took every ounce of strength from Becca, Amy, and me to comfort her.

"Charlene, it's going to be alright. We'll figure this out together," I had whispered through her sobs, holding her trembling body close to mine, sharing her fear and pain. But even then, deep down, I knew our lives would never be the same again.

As I walked away from Erica's bedroom, I couldn't help but let the worry creep into my thoughts. My family, my pack, they were everything to me, and the thought of losing anyone sent a shudder down my spine. I could not let this happen; I would do anything to protect them.

"Love, you look troubled," Nathaniel murmured, wrapping his strong arms around me as I entered our bedroom. His warm embrace brought me a momentary sense of peace.

"Charlene's vision... I can't shake the feeling that something terrible is about to happen," I confessed, burying my face in his chest.

"Hey," he said gently, lifting my chin so our eyes met. "We'll get through this together, just like we always have." I nodded, allowing myself to be comforted by his unwavering faith in us.

"Besides," he continued, a hint of a smile playing on his lips, "you know how stubborn I am. Nothing's going to take me away from you and Erica."

"Stubborn is an understatement," I teased, forcing a smile for his sake.

"Get some sleep, Andriana. We'll face whatever comes together," he whispered, pulling me into bed with him.

The following morning, I stood at the edge of the clearing, watching as Nathaniel, Marshall, and Trenton debated our next steps. Their words were like distant echoes, drowned out by the pounding of my heart.

"Outside help is a risk," Nathaniel argued, his voice tense with apprehension. "But if what Marshall says is true about the Silver Stone pack, it might be worth considering." Marshall nodded, his face a mask of grim determination.

"They've been extending a hand to smaller packs in need, and Declan has taken them under his protection. It could be our best chance at survival." Trenton's jaw clenched, and I knew he was weighing the options carefully. "If we're going to do this, we need to act now. The longer we wait, the more vulnerable we become."

"It's worth considering reaching out to him," Nathaniel said and then Trenton turned to me.

"Isn't that the pack you helped ten years ago, Andriana?" Trenton asked, turning to me. I nodded slowly, remembering how much they had suffered under a dreadful curse. It seemed like a lifetime ago, but I still remembered the look of gratitude in the eyes of the people I had helped.

"Yes, it was. They were good people."

"Then we should reach out to them," Nathaniel said decisively. "We need their help, and I trust Andriana's judgement." I shivered, the cold breeze biting into my skin, and felt the weight of their decision looming over us all. Was it truly the only way to keep our pack safe?

Days later, the Silver Stone pack's emissary, a man by the name of Grayson Thompson who had just been promoted to the Warrior Commander of the Silver Stone pack, arrived at our territory. I watched as Nathaniel and Trenton strode forward to greet him, their posture radiating authority and control.

"Alpha Declan sends his regards," Grayson said. "He's eager to lend assistance to your pack."

"Thank you," Nathaniel replied, his tone cautious yet polite. "We are grateful for your help."

As the negotiations began, I stood off to the side, my fingers nervously twisting the hem of my dress. My heart felt like a caged bird, desperate to escape the suffocating tension that filled the air.

"Are you alright?" Marshall asked, coming to stand beside me. His eyes were kind, but I could see the worry etched into the lines around them.

"I... I don't know," I confessed, swallowing hard. "I can't shake the feeling that something terrible is going to happen. But we have to trust in Nathaniel, and in the Silver Stone pack."

"Indeed," Marshall agreed solemnly. "Our fate now lies in their hands."

The sun dipped low in the sky, casting a warm glow across the Moon Key pack's land as Nathaniel, Trenton, and I stood together near the edge of our territory. My heart pounded in my chest, a mix of hope and fear warring within me. This was the moment we had been waiting for, the day Alpha Declan would contact us.

"Are you sure we can trust them?" Nathaniel asked me as Grayson walked up to the boundary line. I met his gaze, my blue eyes filled with determination.

"Do we really have a choice?" I asked and Nathaniel grimaced.

Trenton stepped forward and greeted Grayson. Grayson smiled and shook Trentons hand.

"Alpha Declan is more than willing to help you. He's offering sanctuary for your werewolves in our pack."

"What about the humans?" Trenton pressed, his protective instincts kicking in.

"Alpha Declan says he can arrange something for the humans as well, but he's not thrilled about having too many of them in such a large pack," Grayson relayed.

I frowned, I understood the risks associated with a large number of humans living amongst werewolves and knew that whilst we weren't the only pack with humans; they were few and far between. Trenton turned and looked at us and Nathaniel made a slight shake of his head. Trenton then turned back to Grayson.

"I appreciate his offer, but we cannot accept it if it means splitting up our pack." Grayson narrowed his eyes as he looked between Trenton and Nathaniel but then shrugged his shoulders with a sigh.

"Are you sure?" he asked and Trenton nodded again. "Well, I will pass the message on. Please reach out if you change your mind." Grayson then turned and disappeared into the woods. A few moments later I heard the sound of a car engine start and then get lower as he drove away.

"Thank you, Trenton," Nathaniel said, placing a hand on his Gamma's shoulder. We all knew that it was awkward to work in this way, but we had all agreed that nobody but our pack knew that Trenton wasn't really the Alpha of our pack.

Three months had passed since our conversation with Alpha Declan's pack, and the air around the Moon Key pack held a mixture of tension and hope. The sun began to set as Trenton approached Nathaniel and me, his eyes filled with determination.

"Alpha Declan has returned," he announced, glancing between us. "He wishes to speak with us." Nathaniel nodded, his expression shifting to one of cautious optimism. As we made our way to the meeting spot, I couldn't help but feel my heart race in anticipation. We desperately needed help, and I could only hope that Alpha Declan had found a way to provide it without tearing our pack apart.

As we reached the clearing, the tall figure of Alpha Declan came into view, his presence commanding attention even from a distance. Beside him stood his son Liam, whose wide-eyed curiosity towards our home was undeniable.

"Alpha Trenton, Gamma Nathaniel," Declan greeted, nodding respectfully. "I have given your situation much thought, and my son here has expressed his fondness for the Moon Key pack."

"Father, they need our help," Liam chimed in earnestly. "We can't just leave them to face the threat alone."

"Quite right," Alpha Declan continued. "Which is why I have come up with a proposal. In exchange for your assistance with managing our pack businesses, we will offer protection to the Moon Key pack with our warriors. This way, your pack remains intact, and we can still lend our aid." Nathaniel's eyes widened slightly, surprise flickering across his face before being replaced with gratitude. He nodded to an excited-looking Trenton who turned back to the Silver Stone pack Alpha.

"Alpha Declan, your generosity is appreciated. We accept your offer."

"Good," Declan said, extending a hand to Trenton. As they shook hands, the weight of their agreement settled upon us all, an understanding that our fates were now intertwined.

"Thank you, Liam," I whispered to Declan's son, my heart swelling with gratitude for his support. "Your empathy for our pack means more than you know."

The warm sunlight bathed the main pack house garden in a golden hue, casting long shadows across the well-tended greenery. Today's meeting had been filled with discussions of trade and mutual protection, and we had finally after seven months come to an arrangement that suited us all. But for the time being, I allowed myself to focus on the laughter and playfulness shared between the children.

Liam, the son of Alpha Declan, and his friend Damon were visiting us once again. I watched as Liam crouched down low, feigning ignorance to Erica's stealthy approach. She moved carefully, her eyes locked onto her target while trying her best to maintain an air of secrecy. It was endearing to see them interact, their bond growing stronger with each visit.

"Nice try, kitten," Liam chuckled, rolling out of the way just in time to avoid Erica's pounce. The amused glint in his eyes was contagious, and I couldn't help but smile as I observed the scene.

"Kitten?" Erica huffed indignantly, puffing out her chest and placing her hands on her hips. "I am not a kitten! I'm a big, fierce wolf!" From the corner of my eye, I noticed Christian sulking by Becca's side. He crossed his arms and muttered something under his breath about Liam being mean to Erica. Becca, ever the voice of reason, scolded Christian gently for his jealousy.

"Christian, it's just harmless fun," she said softly, squeezing his shoulder reassuringly. "Erica is just enjoying some time with new friends." Still clearly disgruntled, Christian made a half-hearted attempt to engage Erica in play. However, she barely spent a minute with him before excitedly bounding off after Liam once more. As I watched, my heart swelled with gratitude for the new connections forming within our pack.

It was nice to have new people around, especially those we could trust. I was relieved that Alpha Declan seemed to hold no memory of Charlene and me from the time we had helped with his curse. Seeing Liam, now ten years old and full of life, served as a reminder that our actions had made a positive impact in the world.

"Hey Luna Becca, Andriana," Liam called out, catching his breath in between fits of laughter. "Thanks for having us over again. We always have a great time."

"Of course, Liam," I replied, my voice warm and genuine. "We're grateful for your friendship and support. It means more than you know."

As the laughter and chatter of our guests slowly faded into the distance, I glanced out the window one last time to see the Silver Stone pack members leaving our territory. My heart felt heavy with the weight of the unspoken tension that seemed to linger in the air, despite their reassuring presence.

"Come on, sweetheart," I said softly to Erica, guiding her towards her bedroom. "It's time for bed."

"Aw, but I'm not tired yet!" she protested, rubbing her eyes. I couldn't help but smile at her stubbornness, she was so much like Nathaniel in that regard.

"Trust me, you will be soon enough," I replied, ruffling her long light red hair affectionately as we entered her room. As I helped her change into her nightclothes, I couldn't shake the feeling that something was off, a sense of unease that gnawed at the edges of my thoughts. I tried to dismiss it, chalking it up to my conversation with Nathaniel over dinner about the new warriors arriving the next day.

"Mummy, when will Liam come back?" Erica asked as I carefully brushed her hair, doing my best to untangle the knots that had formed during her play.

"Hopefully soon, darling," I answered, trying to keep the worry from my voice. "The Silver Stone pack is our ally now, so we'll be seeing more of them." Inside, however, a nagging voice whispered that this newfound protection might not be enough.

"Good," Erica mumbled sleepily, her eyelids drooping. "I like Liam. He's fun. I think I am going to marry him some day." I couldn't help but smile at her innocent words, even as my chest tightened with anxiety. Pulling her into a tight hug, I breathed in her familiar scent, trying to calm my racing thoughts. Erica squirmed slightly but didn't pull away, knowing how much these moments meant to me.

"Alright, into bed you go," I said, finally releasing her. She climbed under the covers, snuggling down and looking so small and vulnerable that it took everything in me not to scoop her back up into my arms.

"Mummy, I love you," she murmured as I leaned in to kiss her forehead tenderly.

"I love you too, Erica. More than anything," I whispered back, my voice thick with emotion. Straightening, I turned off the light and took one last look at my daughter, cocooned in the safety of her bed. Yet the foreboding feeling refused to dissipate, casting a shadow over the peaceful scene before me.

"Goodnight, sweetheart," I said softly, closing the door behind me and leaving her to sleep. As I made my way back to my own room, I couldn't shake the sense that something was coming, and everything after today would be changed forever.

A few hours later, I found myself tossing and turning in bed, unable to shake the unease that plagued me. Despite my best efforts, sleep remained elusive, slipping through my fingers like sand.

Suddenly, my restless night was shattered by a blood-curdling scream that pierced the darkness like a knife. I bolted upright, my heart pounding wildly in my chest as I frantically searched for Nathaniel, but his side of the bed was empty. Where could he be? The dreadful feeling that had followed me throughout the evening intensified tenfold, threatening to crush me beneath its weight. My eyes were drawn to the curtains, where an ominous orange glow flickered menacingly, casting eerie shadows on the walls. With trembling hands, I pushed the curtains aside to reveal the source of the light – our home, our sanctuary, was engulfed in flames.

"Goddess, no," I whispered, horror-stricken.

The bedroom door slammed open, making me jump. Nathaniel burst into the room, sweat dripping from his brow and terror etched across his face. His panicked gaze swept over the bed, then the rest of the room, before finally landing on me, relief flooding his features.

"Quick, get Erica, we're under attack!"

Chapter 15

Erica - 5 years old

Panic clawed at my chest as I stumbled through the dark woods, my heart pounding in my ears. The branches from the trees and bushes whipped against my skin, scratching me and tearing at my clothes. My breath came out in ragged gasps, and I was so cold, wet, and muddy from all the times I had fallen over.

"Mummy!" I cried out, tears streaming down my face. My mummy had pulled me out of bed earlier, telling me that we needed to run for the safehouse. She didn't say why, or what was happening. All I knew was that pain and fear wrapped around me like a suffocating blanket.

As I ran, I could hear the horrifying screams of people in pain and the sounds of crashing through the woods. The orange-yellow glow of flames flickered on the edges of my vision, lighting up houses near the woods. My heart ached with the need to find my mummy and be safe in her arms again. I had tried to follow the pack's school teacher and the other children when we fled, but I tripped and fell behind. Now I was alone, terrified, and desperate to find my mummy.

"Mummy, where are you?" I sobbed, my voice barely audible over the chaos around me. Every shadow seemed to take on a menacing form, my imagination running wild with monsters lurking in the darkness.

Memories of bedtime stories about big, scary creatures hiding in the woods flooded my mind, making it even harder to keep going. But I couldn't stop; I had to find my mummy.

Panic coursed through my veins as I continued to stumble through the dark woods, desperately searching for my mummy. My heart pounded in my chest, and I could barely catch my breath as I tripped over roots and branches hidden among the shadows. The cold air stung my cheeks, and the wet ground beneath me seemed intent on pulling me down with every step.

"Mummy!" I cried out again, hoping she was close. My voice sounded small and scared, swallowed up by the night around me.

Suddenly, I heard a low, guttural snarl behind me. Fear seized my body, forcing me to turn. My eyes met those of a large black wolf, its golden glowing eyes locked onto me. I could tell it was an Alpha, but not Alpha Trenton from my pack. This wolf was different, foreign, and terrifying.

"Mummy!" I screamed, the sound barely escaping my lips as terror gripped my throat. Desperate to escape the menacing beast, I tried to back away, but my foot caught on something in the dark. I realised too late that it was another wolf, smaller and lying low to the ground. Tripping over the wolf, I fell hard onto my back, the cold, wet earth pressing against me.

The large black wolf seemed poised to lunge, a sight I had seen before when watching the older wolves in our pack train for battle. But I was only five years old, I was too young for training, and this big scary wolf wasn't one of ours.

"Please, no," I whimpered, tears streaming down my face as I stared up at the fierce creature, praying for someone, anyone, to save me.

"Mummy, please help me!" I cried out once more, hoping beyond hope that she would hear me and come to my rescue.

Just as the monstrous black wolf prepared to pounce on me, another black wolf burst into view, its powerful form colliding with the terrifying attacker. Relief washed over me as I recognised the newcomer as my father, his strong body successfully knocking the enemy away from me.

"Erica!" a familiar voice called out desperately. My mother's arms wrapped around me, pulling me to my feet and sheltering me behind her. "It's okay, baby girl, I've got you." Her voice trembled, but her grip was firm and comforting.

"Help!" she shouted, her voice filled with urgency. "Amy!" My Aunt Amy appeared by my mother's side in an instant, her eyes wide with fear.

"Andriana, what happened?"

"Take Erica to the safe house," my mother ordered, her voice laced with authority despite her distress. "Don't let anything happen to her."

"Mummy, I want to stay with you!" I screamed, clutching at her arm as tears streamed down my face. The world seemed to have gone mad, and all I wanted was to stay close to my parents, who always made me feel safe.

"Sweetheart, you need to go with Aunt Amy, she'll keep you safe," my mother whispered, her voice cracking as she tried to hide her own fear. "I love you so much, Erica. Now go."

"Keep her safe, Amy," my mother said, her gaze locked onto my auntie as she entrusted her precious daughter to her care.

"Of course," Amy replied, her voice thick with emotion. She took my hand and began to lead me away from the chaotic scene. All I wanted was to stay with my mother, to be enveloped in her protective embrace.

But I had no choice but to follow my aunt, my tiny hand gripping hers tightly.

"Mummy!" I wailed one last time, craning my neck to catch a glimpse of her as we moved away from the battle. She stood tall, waving her arms in urgent movements, coordinating the defenders as my father continued to fight the menacing Alpha.

"Come on, Erica," Amy urged, pulling me around a tree and out of sight of my mother. The sounds of fighting grew fainter as we put distance between ourselves and the chaos, but the fear in my heart only grew stronger.

"Please, Aunt Amy," I whimpered, "I want my mummy."

"I know, sweetheart," she replied gently, squeezing my hand reassuringly. "But right now, we need to get you to safety."

We dashed through the woods, my small legs struggling to keep up with Aunt Amy's long strides. My heart pounded in my chest as we ran, and fear gripped me like a vice. The cold night air stung my cheeks, and the shadows of the trees seemed to reach out for me like grasping hands.

"Almost there, sweetheart," Aunt Amy panted, her eyes wide and filled with worry. As we reached the entrance to the safe house, the sight that met us was one of pure horror. My school teacher lay lifeless on the ground, her body twisted in an unnatural angle. Several other pack members were scattered around her, their once vibrant faces now deathly pale. The entrance to the safe house was engulfed in flames, the heat so intense that it felt like I was standing too close to the sun.

"Miss Jenkins!" I cried, tears streaming down my face as I caught sight of my beloved teacher. "What happened to her?"

"Shh, Erica," Aunt Amy whispered, her own eyes brimming with tears. She pulled me closer to her side, shielding me from the gruesome scene.

"But Aunt Amy, why is Miss Jenkins—"

"Sweetie, I need you to be brave, okay?" Aunt Amy interrupted, her voice cracking. "I promise, I'll do everything I can to protect you. But right now, we have to keep moving."

"Where are we going?" My voice trembled as I looked up at her, searching for some sense of reassurance.

"Somewhere safe, baby girl," she said, gently wiping away my tears with her thumb. "There's a place by the lake where we can hide until this is all over." She took my hand and led me back into the woods, away from the burning safe house and the bodies of our fallen pack mates. The sounds of crashing branches and distant screams continued to haunt us as we ran, each one adding another layer of fear to the already terrifying night.

"Stay close, Erica," Aunt Amy urged me, her eyes darting around nervously. "We're going to make it through this together."

As Aunt Amy led me away from the safe house, the ground beneath my feet grew increasingly uneven and treacherous. The cold mud squelched around my small shoes, causing me to slip and stumble with each step. My heartbeat pounded in my ears, drowning out the distant sounds of chaos that still echoed through the woods.

"Be careful, Erica," Aunt Amy called over her shoulder as we neared the lake. "The ground gets slippery here." I tried to heed her warning, but my foot suddenly caught on a root, sending me tumbling to the ground. My grip on Amy's hand slipped, and I found myself alone and disoriented in the damp forest.

"Aunt Amy!" I cried out, my voice cracking from fear and exhaustion. Panic threatened to consume me as I scrambled to my feet, searching desperately for my aunt's familiar figure.

"Erica!" Amy shouted back, her voice coming from the edge of a steep hill overlooking the lake. Relief washed over me as I spotted her standing there, her arms outstretched, beckoning me to join her. But before I could call out to her, a massive wolf lunged at her from the shadows, its teeth bared and eyes glowing with malevolent intent.

"AMY!" I screamed, my heart feeling like it was being ripped apart as she disappeared from view. Her agonised screams filled the air, followed by snarls and growls that made my blood run cold.

Determined to reach her, I tried to climb the slippery hill, digging my fingers into the wet earth in an attempt to gain purchase. But the more I struggled, the more I slid back down, tears of frustration streaming down my face.

"Please... I need to help her," I sobbed, choking on my words. But just as I was about to cry out for Amy again, a hand clamped over my mouth, muffling my screams.

"Shh," a familiar voice whispered in my ear. "It's okay, Erica. You're safe now." Recognising the voice as Christian, I stopped struggling and turned to hug him tightly, my small body shaking uncontrollably.

He was one of my favourite people in the pack, and I trusted him completely.

"Christian," I sobbed into his shoulder, my voice barely audible. "Aunt Amy... there was a wolf..."

"I know," he said softly, his face filled with concern and sorrow. "I'm so sorry, Erica. But right now, I need you to be strong. Can you do that for me?" I nodded against his chest, trying to hold back more tears. As much as I wanted to find Aunt Amy, I knew that if Christian said we needed to stay hidden, then it must be for a good reason.

"Promise you'll protect me?" I whispered, my voice trembling.

"Always," he replied, his voice determined and unwavering. "I promise, no matter what happens, I'll keep you safe." And though the world around us was crumbling, and my heart ached for my family, I found solace in Christian's arms, trusting that he would be my shield against the darkness.

"Come on, we need to keep moving," Christian whispered urgently, helping me up the slippery hillside. As we reached the top, I noticed his eyes widen in shock at something beyond my view.

"Christian, what is it?" I asked, my heart pounding in my chest. I tried to peek around him, but he quickly turned to face me, offering a strained smile.

"Nothing you need to worry about, little one," he said, though I could tell he was lying. "Now close your eyes; I'm going to carry you for a bit." I hesitated for a moment before obeying, squeezing my eyelids shut tight as he lifted me into his arms. The steady rhythm of his footsteps did little to calm my racing thoughts, and I couldn't resist the urge to open my eyes and look over his shoulder.

And that's when I saw her, Aunt Amy, lying motionless on the ground, her body twisted unnaturally. My breath caught in my throat as tears welled up in my eyes once more. Why was everything going wrong?

"Christian..." I choked out, my voice barely above a whisper. He glanced back at me, his expression pained, and then shifted me in his arms so I couldn't see the horror behind us.

"Please, don't look," he pleaded softly. "I know it's hard, Erica, but you have to stay strong. Just focus on holding onto me, okay?" I nodded numbly, wrapping my small arms tightly around his neck as he continued to carry me through the nightmarish woods.

Chapter 16

Erica

"Almost there, Erica," Christian whispered urgently as he navigated through the dense trees and rocky outcroppings. He finally reached a small opening in the woods, hidden from view by the towering cliffs and foliage. This was the Hollow, a place my parents used to tell me stories about when I was tucked safely into bed. It was supposed to be magical, but tonight it only felt eerie and foreboding. As we entered, a strange pop sounded in my ears, and suddenly, the screams and fighting that had haunted us for what seemed like forever ceased. The abrupt silence was almost as terrifying as the chaos that had preceded it. Christian moved towards the furthest corner of the Hollow and gently placed me down behind one of the large stones that formed a mysterious circle at its centre. My heart still pounded in my chest, and I fought back the tears that threatened to spill over once more.

"Shh, we have to be really quiet, okay?" Christian warned, his own voice trembling slightly. "I won't leave you, Erica. I promise. I'll protect you even until my last dying breath." His words sounded odd, like something Daddy would say to Uncle Trenton or Uncle Marshall during their serious talks. But despite their strangeness, they brought me some comfort. I trusted Christian, if anyone could keep me safe, it was him.

"Please don't go," I begged, tears streaming down my cheeks as I clung desperately to his arm.

"I'm not going anywhere," he reassured me, his hand brushing away my tears before settling on my shoulder. "Just stay close and stay quiet, alright?" Nodding, I scooted closer to Christian, seeking solace in his presence amidst the darkness that had swallowed our world. The Hollow's shadows loomed around us like silent guardians, watching our every move with bated breath.

For a moment, we sat there in the stillness, my small frame pressed against his side as we both listened to the eerie silence. I couldn't help but think about Aunt Amy, her lifeless body, a haunting image that refused to leave my mind. Would we ever be safe again? Would the night ever end?

"Christian," I whispered, my voice barely audible. "Do you think everyone else is okay?"

"I hope so, Erica," he replied quietly, his grip on my shoulder tightening. "We just have to believe that they're all going to be alright."

The earth beneath us trembled, sending a shiver down my spine. My breath hitched as I turned to Christian, searching for an explanation. But his gaze was fixed on the entrance of the Hollow, where a strange glow had appeared.

"What's happening?" I whispered, my voice quivering with fear. The rumbling grew louder, shaking the ground beneath us more violently.

"Shit! Stay behind me," Christian instructed, his eyes never leaving the source of the light. He stood tall in front of me, shielding me from whatever was coming. As another rumble echoed through the Hollow, the glow suddenly burst inwards like a thousand suns. I squinted against the brightness, trying to make sense of the chaos that unfolded before us.

Unfamiliar werewolves, in both human and wolf form, stormed into our hiding place. Their snarls and growls filled the air, drowning out the pounding of my heart. Christian's back tensed, his fists clenched at his sides as he kept me hidden from their sight.

"Christian, who are they?" I whimpered, my small fingers gripping the fabric of his shirt.

"Enemies," he muttered under his breath, his voice strained. "Don't worry, Erica. I won't let them hurt you." I peeked around him, my curiosity getting the better of me despite my fear. The intruders' eyes were wild and ruthless, their faces twisted in anger and hate. They didn't belong here, in our secret sanctuary. They were a storm, crashing through our world and leaving destruction in their wake.

"Promise me you'll stay quiet," Christian whispered urgently, his gaze locked on the invading werewolves. "No matter what happens, don't make a sound." I nodded solemnly, too afraid to speak. Tears welled up in my eyes as I pressed myself closer to him, needing his warmth and strength to keep me grounded in the midst of the chaos.

"Promise," I whispered back, my voice barely audible. Christian gave me a reassuring smile before turning his attention back to the intruders.

A snarl echoed through the Hollow, and suddenly Christian was no longer in front of me. My heart skipped a beat as I watched him fly through the air, crashing into the cliff wall with a sickening thud.

"Christian!" I screamed, but he didn't move, his body crumpled on the ground.

"Please get up," I whispered, tears spilling down my cheeks. But he didn't hear me; he was too far away now. A man appeared before me, walking slowly through the chaos. He had an air of authority, and the other werewolves seemed to cower in his presence. As he came closer, I couldn't help but feel a sense of dread settle over me. He was the eye of the storm, the dark centre around which all this destruction swirled.

He stopped before me and knelt down, his face inches from mine. His grip on my chin was tight, almost painful, as if he was trying to squeeze the fear out of me. I tried to pull away, but he held on tighter, the pressure sending sharp jolts of pain through my jaw.

"Let me go," I whispered through clenched teeth, but he ignored me, his icy blue eyes flecked with copper boring into mine.

"Hello there, well aren't you precious?" The man's sneering smile widened as he gripped my chin. I tried to pull away again, but his iron fingers refused to let me go. "You will make a fine mate for my son," he said, and my heart filled with dread.

I didn't know who this man was or who his son could be, but I knew I didn't want to be his son's mate. Even at my young age, I understood the concept of fated mates, and I was far too young for mine right now.

"Such a precious little thing," he said, his voice cold and cruel. "You've got spirit, that's for sure."

"Leave her alone!" Christian's voice rang out, though it sounded weak and strained. The man glanced in his direction, amusement flickering across his features.

"Or what?" he taunted, smirking. "You're in no position to make demands, boy."

"Christian..." I murmured, desperate to help him but unsure of what I could do. The man tightened his grip on my chin, making me wince.

"Quiet," he hissed, his breath hot and foul against my face.

"Please," I begged, my voice shaking. "I just want my mummy. I want to go home."

"Home?" the man asked, his smile twisted. "You'll have a new home soon enough. One where you'll learn your place." He turned his attention back to Christian, who was struggling to push himself up from the ground. "And as for you...well, you should know better than to stand in my way."

"Leave her alone!" Christian yelled again, his voice strained with pain and anger. "If you hurt her, I'll kill you!" The man just laughed, an icy sound that sent shivers down my spine. He turned to one of the other men and said,

"Shut that mutt up."

My heart skipped a beat as I heard Christian scream in agony. I tried to see him, but the bad man had blocked my view as he picked me up, cradling me against his chest like a twisted mockery of a father's embrace. He began to carry me out of the Hollow, away from Christian and everything I knew.

"Christian!" I screamed, struggling against the man's grip. But it was no use - his arms were like steel, and I couldn't break free.

"Be quiet, little girl," the man growled, his breath hot against my ear. "Your fate is sealed."

I wriggled and squirmed, trying to break free from the man's iron grip. He was a strong Alpha, I could tell, but I couldn't give up. I had to try to escape no matter what. As we passed through the entrance of the Hollow, my ears popped and the horrifying sounds of screams and fighting flooded back in.

"Let me go!" I cried, tears streaming down my face. The man only chuckled darkly, making my stomach churn with terror.

"Keep this up, little pup," he snarled, "and you'll wish I'd left you to die."

"Leave her alone!" a familiar voice shouted, piercing through the chaos. I strained to see past the man, my heart leaping as I saw Beta Marshall running towards us. Hope surged through me, but it was short-lived.

Suddenly, I felt like I was flying, weightless and terrified. The sensation lasted only a moment before pain exploded in my head as I crashed into a wall. My vision blurred, and I realised that both the man and I had been thrown against the cliff side.

"Erica!" Beta Marshall called out, his voice laced with concern as he sprinted towards me. I could barely focus on him, my head throbbing with pain. I clutched at the cold, jagged stones, desperate to ground myself in reality.

"Mar-Mar..." I whimpered, using the nickname I'd given him when I was younger. I wanted so badly for him to scoop me up and take me away from this nightmare, but the man still stood between us, his expression twisted with rage.

"Stay away from her," the bad Alpha spat, pushing himself off the wall with a menacing growl. "You were warned what would happen if you kept her from me."

"Over my dead body," Beta Marshall snarled back, his eyes locked on mine for a brief moment, filled with fierce determination and love.

"Your wish is my command," the man sneered, and I felt a cold wave of dread wash over me as he lunged at Marshall.

The pain in my head pulsed like a drumbeat as I struggled to focus on my surroundings. My mummy's face appeared above me, her eyes dark with concern.

"Erica, sweetheart, are you okay?" she asked, her voice barely audible over the chaos.

"Mummy..." I whispered, my voice weak and shaky. She forced a smile, but I could see the fear beneath it. Before I could say anything else, I saw my daddy in wolf form, along with Alpha Trenton and Beta Marshall, surrounding the bad Alpha man who had hurt me. The tension in the air was palpable, and I couldn't help but let out a scream as my daddy lunged at the enemy.

"NO!" I cried, watching helplessly as the bad Alpha caught my daddy by the throat. A horrible cracking sound echoed through the night, and my daddy went limp, his lifeless body crumpling to the ground.

"NOOO!" I wailed, tears streaming down my face. My heart felt like it was being torn apart as I watched my daddy, my protector, fall before my eyes.

My mummy's own scream of agony pierced the air, and she clutched her chest, her face twisted with pain. She must have felt Daddy's death, their bond snapping like a fragile thread. Her gaze locked onto mine, and she mouthed the words "I love you" before pressing a tender kiss to my forehead.

"Be strong, my little one," she whispered, her voice strained with emotion. Then, she turned away from me and stalked towards the bad Alpha, a strange glow enveloping her as she moved.

"Mummy, no!" I screamed, my vision starting to blur as black spots danced before my eyes. My head throbbed with each beat of my heart, and I could feel myself slipping away from consciousness.

"Mummy, please!" I sobbed, reaching out for her with my small, trembling hands. But it was too late. The black spots grew larger, swallowing up the world around me until nothing remained but darkness.

"Mummy..." I whispered one last time, before the darkness claimed me completely.

My eyes fluttered open, and I was greeted by the silence that enveloped the dimly lit room. The only sounds permeating the quiet were hushed voices and soft crying. My heart ached as I called out, my voice barely above a whisper,

"Mummy?"

Luna Becca rushed to my side, tears staining her cheeks. She pulled me into a warm embrace, her body trembling with sobs. I glanced around the room, seeing Alpha Trenton, Beta Marshall, Charlene, and the sleeping twin babies huddled together in the shadows.

"Rest, sweetheart," Luna Becca urged, gently laying me back down on the makeshift bed. As sleep began to tug at my consciousness, fragments of conversation drifted to my ears. My chest tightened as I heard the words: Christian, Amy, and my parents... gone. The pack territory was ruined by fire. The people in this room were all that remained, and they needed to find safety. Alpha Trenton's voice was firm as he spoke,

"Protecting her is our top priority."

I didn't know who he meant, but his words brought a small measure of comfort amidst the chaos. My eyelids grew heavy as sleep finally claimed me once more, pulling me under its dark embrace.

BOUND BY FATE

CONTINUE ERICA'S STORY IN...

Bound by Fate

The Key Stone Pack – Book 1

In a world filled with ancient prophecies and deadly rivalries, Erica, a rogue werewolf unable to shift, despises everything about Alphas. But destiny has other plans for her as she discovers she is the fated mate of Liam, a cursed alpha with a haunting past. When tragedy strikes, Erica's only choice is to escape the town that holds painful memories.

However, fate's cruel hand intervenes once more When Liam learns of Erica's plans he resorts to desperate measures to bind their fates. As Liam tries to convince Erica of their destined love, another alpha, Jasper, with a dangerous grudge against Liam, stands in their way. Jasper's thirst for power and revenge threatens to unravel the delicate threads of fate, and Erica finds herself torn between trust, loyalty, and her fearsome attraction to Liam.

In this gripping tale of dark paranormal romance, will Erica succumb to the fate written in the stars, or will she forge her path, defying the ominous prophecy? As passion mingles with danger, and love battles against malevolence, the web of secrets and lies tightens. Dive into a world where love is intertwined with darkness, and nothing is as it seems.

Available on Paperback, Kindle and Kindle Unlimited from 4th September 2023

You can find it here – books2read.com/TKSPBBF

About Aisling Elizabeth

Hey there! I'm **Aisling Elizabeth** (yep, that's pronounced ASH-Ling). A Yorkshire lass through and through, I juggle the fun chaos of two kids and two mischievous cats while weaving my genius masterpieces. I've always been the storytelling type. Before getting my name on an actual book cover in 2022, I dabbled with sharing my tales on reading apps. Turned out, people kinda liked them!

Dark paranormal romance is my thing. In my stories, you'll find threads of resilience in the face of tough times, characters whose lives are all tangled up (in the best way), and some nods to mental health – something close to my heart, given my own ups and downs.

My first published piece? "Beyond Beta's Rejection", kicking off The Divine Order Series. But trust me, my brain's always buzzing with a bunch of new story ideas.

Outside of spinning tales, I'm all about belting out songs (quality not guaranteed), hopping into gigs, and geeking out at TV and Film fan conventions. If you share my love for any of the above, we'll get on just fine!

If you want to see more of me, or spend time with me (I can't promise I won't sing) then check the links below.

Website - www.aislingelizabeth.com

Facebook Reader Group – www.aislingelizabeth.com/puzzlepieces

Also By Aisling Elizabeth

Current and Future Releases

The Divine Order Series
Beyond Beta's Rejection
The Alpha's Tainted Blood
The Gamma's Shattered Soul *(coming soon)*

The Key Stone Pack Series
Bound by Prophecy *(Prequel)*

Bound by Fate
Bound by Rivalry *(coming soon)*
Bound by Curse *(coming soon)*

Dark Heath University
Dark Ashes *(Prequel) (coming soon)*
Dark Flame *(coming soon)*
Dark Inferno *(coming soon)*

Claimed by the Curse the Series
Claimed by the Pack *(coming soon)*

Printed in Great Britain
by Amazon